Genevra Sisson Snedden

Docas, the Indian Boy of Santa Clara

Genevra Sisson Snedden

Docas, the Indian Boy of Santa Clara

ISBN/EAN: 9783337057428

Printed in Europe, USA, Canada, Australia, Japan

Cover: Foto ©Andreas Hilbeck / pixelio.de

More available books at **www.hansebooks.com**

DOCAS

THE INDIAN BOY OF SANTA CLARA

BY

GENEVRA SISSON SNEDDEN

D. C. HEATH & CO., PUBLISHERS

BOSTON   NEW YORK   CHICAGO

My dear Children: —

What sort of people do you like best to read about — white people or Indians?

I think you will say Indians, because all the children of whom I have ever asked this question have said that they liked best to read about Indians. Indians do everything so differently from the way we do that they are always interesting.

This book which we are now going to read is about Indians, — the Indians who lived near the Pacific Ocean before our grandfathers were born, and before we Americans came west and settled the country.

Do you like best to read about grown-up people or about children? I think I can hear you say, "What a question! Children, of course!" Yes, children can have such fun, running and playing and finding out about all kinds of things for which grown people never have time, that it is much pleasanter to read about them. So this whole book is about children. The first part tells about the little Indian boy, Docas; farther on, when Docas grows to be a man, the book tells about his children and grandchildren.

Last of all, the stories tell about things that actually happened to Indian children long ago in California, so they are what you call "truly stories," not "made-up ones."

These are some of the reasons why the children for whom the stories were first written liked them and learned from them, and for these same reasons I think many of you will care to read about Docas, the Indian boy of Santa Clara.

THE AUTHOR.

NOTE.

These stories were originally written to serve as reading material for the children in the University School connected with the Department of Education at the Leland Stanford Junior University. The never-failing delight with which those children welcomed each new instalment was the first impetus toward putting the stories in a form where they would have a larger audience.

The work was done as a thesis in history under the direction of Mary Sheldon Barnes. To her careful supervision and many suggestions the book owes much of whatever merit it may possess.

TABLE OF CONTENTS.

PART I.

WHEN DOCAS LIVED AT THE INDIAN VILLAGE.

PART II.

WHEN DOCAS LIVED AT THE MISSION.

PART III.

WHEN DOCAS LIVED WITH DON SECUNDINI ROBLES.

PART I.

WHEN DOCAS LIVED AT THE INDIAN VILLAGE.

A little Indian boy poked his head out of a brush house.

PART I.

BUILDING THE FIRE.

"OH, mother!" cried a little Indian boy, "I am hungry."

" Then go and start the fire so that I can cook breakfast," answered his mother.

It was about a hundred years ago that this little boy, whose name was Docas, poked his head out of a brush house. Ama, his mother, was sitting on the ground just outside, grinding acorns in a stone bowl.

Docas went to the middle of the hut, where the blazing fire of wood had been the night before. Just before Ama had gone tc sleep she had covered with ashes the glowing coals that were left from the fire.

Docas raked off the ashes and began to blow on the blackened coals that were left. There was not much life in them, but they began to redden a little.

He put some dry leaves against them and blew

3

harder. The leaves smoked, but would not light, no matter how hard he blew. And all the time the coals were getting blacker and blacker.

At last he called, "I cannot light it, mother."

Ama came over where he was and began to blow, too; but even she could not start it, for the fire had died out.

"I must get some new fire," said Ama at last.

She picked up two dry willow sticks and two flints. She rubbed the willow sticks together very hard for a while.

"Do you see the little dust that is gathering?" she asked. "Now I will strike the flints together until they send a spark down into that dry dust."

In a few minutes a spark fell into the dust, the dust flared up, and Docas exclaimed, "There! now we have a fire." He dropped some dry leaves on the burning dust, then he put some little twigs on the leaves. After that he called to his younger brother: —

"Wake up, Heema! Come and get some big sticks for the fire."

Heema rolled off the mat of tule reeds on which he had been sleeping, rubbed his eyes, and said, "I'm ready, Docas."

Heema did not have to spend time dressing. All the Indian children ever wore was a little skirt made of rabbit-skin or deer-skin.

In a minute more Heema had piled some large sticks on the fire. Then it blazed up brightly.

" It's foggy, and I'm cold," said Docas. " Sit down by the fire with me and get warm."

Docas and Heema were California Indians. They lived in an Indian rancheria, or village, near San Francisco Bay. Their father, whose name was Massea, was chief of the rancheria.

Docas was seven years old, while Heema was six. Alachu, one of their sisters, was three. Umwa was the other sister. She was so tiny that she had to be carried in a basket on her mother's back.

DOCAS AT BREAKFAST.

" PUT the stones into the fire, boys, so that they will be hot when the acorns are ground," said Ama.

Docas pulled toward the fire five large stones that were lying near.

" I'll throw them in," said Heema, tossing them into the middle of the hottest blaze.

Then Docas said, " Let's surprise father by shooting a rabbit for breakfast."

" Here are your bow and arrows," answered Heema.

In a moment more they ran off. Docas hunted among the brush and trees near by for a rabbit, but he could not find one, so he ran back toward the rancheria.

"I've found something that's better than rabbits," Docas heard Heema say suddenly.

"Where are you, Heema?" asked Docas.

"Here among the bushes, eating thimble-berries," answered Heema, peeping out from among the large green leaves.

Docas laughed and began eating berries, too. The berries were so good that they forgot all about breakfast, until suddenly they heard their mother's voice calling: —

"Boys, where are you? The acorns are ready to cook."

The boys took one last mouthful of thimble-berries and then bounded toward the rancheria.

Ama put a basketful of cold water down by the fire as they came up.

"Heema, pour the acorn meal into the water. Docas, rake out the hot stones and put them into the water to cook the mush," said Ama.

"I hope this mush will not be bitter," said Docas, as he dropped a red-hot stone into the water.

"No; this will be good, for I soaked the acorns a long time and then dried them in the sun before I ground them," answered Ama.

In a few minutes the mush was cooked; then Ama called Massea, and the whole family sat around the basket. They all ate out of it at once, using sticks hollowed out at the end in stead of spoons.

HOW DOCAS WENT FISHING.

ONE day Massea came up to Docas.

"To-day we will go fishing," he said.

Then Docas ran away to find his playmates.

"We are going fishing! We are going fishing!" he cried.

Then all the children began to dance and jump.

"We are going fishing! We are going fishing!" they screamed. For the children were glad when the fishing days came.

But first Massea must drive stakes across the bed of the creek just below the boys' swimming hole.

And he must drive them very close together, for he wants to keep the fish from swimming through.

After Massea had made the fence, Docas called to Heema, "I'll race you up the creek."

"You will have to hurry or I shall beat you," answered Heema.

Then they both started to run along the bank of the creek.

"Come, Alachu. You may go, too," said Ama.

All the women and children in the rancheria went also. They walked along the bank of the creek for about a quarter of a mile, then Alachu cried, "I see Docas. I see Heema."

Docas was standing on the bank. "Watch me!" he called to Alachu.

He dived off the bank and disappeared in a large hole.

"Mother! mother! Docas is drowned!" cried Alachu.

Ama smiled and answered, "Wait and see."

In a minute more Docas's head popped suddenly out of the water.

Then the women and children walked out into the middle of the creek and began to wade down it.

Alachu heard a shout and saw Heema getting ready to jump.

"Be careful; I am afraid you will jump on top of me," she cried.

There was a big splash, and Alachu gave a scream as the water splashed over her. Heema was standing in the water a few feet away.

"A water fight! We'll have a water fight!" cried the children.

They jumped about in the water. They splashed it all over each other. They laughed and shouted and made all the noise they could.

"Then we will spear them."

As they stopped for a moment to take breath, Docas said, "See the fish swim down the creek. They are scared."

The battle lasted until the rancheria was in sight, and by that time all the fish were in the swimming hole. Then Massea said, "Now we must build a fence above them."

When the fence was built, Docas said, "Now the fish cannot swim away, for there is a fence below them and a fence above them."

That night Massea said, "We will build fires on the bank of the creek. The fish will come near to look at the light; then we will spear them."

And so it happened. The men speared enough fish that night to give them something to eat for several days.

MASSEA'S STOREHOUSE.

ONE day in October, Massea said to Docas, "Come, Docas, you must help me make a storehouse to-day, so that we shall have something to eat by and by."

Massea and Docas went out into the woods. They hunted until they found an oak tree with two branches growing straight out at about the same height from the ground.

Massea said, "Climb the tree, Docas;" so Docas scrambled up.

Massea then handed him some straight sticks. Docas put these sticks across from branch to branch, and tied the ends fast to the two branches of the tree with deerskin strings. After this his father brought up some twigs that bent easily. They wove these back and forth among the sticks until they had a good floor for their storehouse. In the same way they made the sides and the top, leaving a hole near the trunk of the tree for a door.

After the storehouse was made, Docas said to some of the other little Indian children, " Let's go off and get some acorns to put in the storehouse."

They took their baskets and went off toward the hills, Soon they came to some big oak trees.

One of the little boys called out, " Look! the ground is covered with acorns under that tree."

Sure enough, the acorns had dropped down from the tree until they were so thick on the ground that the children could scrape them up. Before night they had filled their baskets.

Docas put the acorns he had gathered into the storehouse which he and his father had made. Every day the children went out to gather acorns; every night they poured them into the storehouse, and soon it was full.

The day they finished filling it, Docas saw a little squirrel run up the trunk of the tree and go into the storehouse. Docas stood very still and watched. In a few minutes he saw the squirrel come back with his cheeks sticking out. He was carrying off the acorns.

Docas ran over to where his father was lying in the shade of a large tree, and said, " Oh, father, we shall not have any acorns left in a few days. The squirrels have begun to carry them off."

Massea went over to the tree in which the storehouse was built. He smeared a broad band of pitch clear around the trunk.

" This will stop them," he said.

The Indians had no more trouble after that; for if anything tried to climb the tree, it was caught in the band of sticky pitch.

While Massea was smearing the pitch around the trunk, Docas saw a bird at work in a tree near by.

' " There is the woodpecker," cried Docas, pointing to a woodpecker busily putting acorns away in his storehouse.

The woodpecker's storehouse was not like Massea's Every summer the woodpecker pecks a great many holes just the size of an acorn in the bark of a tree. When fall comes, and the acorns are ripe, he puts the best ones in his holes. He hammers them in so tight that they do not often fall out.

After the storehouse was made.

"I hope we shall not have to take the woodpecker's .acorns this winter," said Massea.

As long as their acorns lasted, Massea and the other Indians did not touch the acorns that the woodpecker had gathered. But one day all the Indians at the rancheria went off fishing. While they were gone their campfire spread and burned the tree in which they had made their storehouse.

Docas was skipping along ahead as they came home. He saw what had happened. He ran back to Massea and Ama, crying out, "The storehouse is burnt! The storehouse is burnt!"

Massea looked very sad at supper that night, and said, "I am afraid we shall have to take the woodpeckers' acorns."

The Indians did not like to take the acorns, so they waited three days. By that time they were so hungry that they could wait no longer.

Docas built a fire near the woodpecker's tree. The smoke that went up from it told the woodpecker that he would have to go. After a little he did not care to stay, for the smoke spoiled the acorns for him. So he flew away.

Docas then climbed the tree and pulled off the bark. That let the acorns fall out and then the Indians gathered them up and put them into a new storehouse, ready for future use.

HOW DOCAS CAUGHT THE GRASSHOPPERS.

ONE day in September, Docas and the rest of the family were all seated round a large basket. They were eating their acorn mush. Just as Docas put his stick in to get some, he heard something go "click" behind him.

He thought to himself, "The grasshoppers are getting thicker."

He lifted his stick, and there in the mush on the end of it was a grasshopper.

"Look!" said Docas to Heema.

"Let me get him out," said Heema, laughing and picking up a stick from the ground. Heema lifted the grasshopper out of the mush.

Then Docas said, "Let's catch grasshoppers to-morrow."

Heema said, "Yes."

All day they heard the "Click, click," of jumping grasshoppers.

That evening, when the children began playing, Docas ran up to them and said, "Help me dig a hole to catch the grasshoppers in."

The children began digging a little way out from the rancheria, and before dark they had made a big hole.

Next morning, while the grasshoppers were still cold and stiff, Docas said to the children,

" Let's make a big ring around the hole before the sun warms the grasshoppers."

And they did so.

"Now we will walk slowly toward the hole," said the children.

Little by little the children came nearer. Little by little the ring grew smaller. Little by little the grasshoppers inside the ring grew frightened.

"They're jumping down into the hole now," said Docas.

Soon the children were close to the edge of the hole.

" I am going to jump into the hole," said Docas. " I can soon catch them down there. They cannot jump out so easily as they jumped in."

So Docas caught all the grasshoppers that were in the hole. He longed to eat them, but he waited until they were cooked. Ama baked the grasshoppers in the fire until they were quite dry; then she ground them in the stone bowl just as she did the acorns.

After that the Indians ate them.

THE GRASS-SEED BASKET.

ONE morning in spring, Ama said to Docas, "Stir up the fire. I must get breakfast."

"I shall have to get some sticks," answered Docas, running off to the woods.

Baby Umwa was playing near. "Baby will make a big fire for mother," she thought.

She began picking up dry leaves and throwing them on the fire. "Here are some good sticks," she said to herself.

Docas had dropped his bow and arrows on the ground. She picked them up and threw them on the blazing leaves; then she picked up a basket and threw it on also.

"Hurry, Docas! See baby's big fire!"

Docas rushed forward and seized the blazing basket, but it was so badly burned that it could not be used.

"Umwa! Umwa!" he cried. "You silly little baby! Mother will have to work for weeks to make her basket for grass-seed again."

Ama felt very sorry when she saw the burnt basket.

"You must go to-day and get some more roots with which to make some new baskets," she said.

After breakfast Docas and Heema went down to the edge of the bay.

" How are you going to dig up the roots? "
asked Heema.

" With my toes," answered Docas.

The long round roots ran along just under the
ground in the mud.   Docas stuck his bare toes
into the mud, wriggling them along under a root.
He loosened it a little at each wriggle, and by and
by he pulled up a long straight root.

Heema helped also, and that evening they carried home a big bundle of roots.

The next day they went up in the hills and
gathered a large number of maidenhair ferns.
They came back by the San Francisquito creek
and broke off a great many willow branches.

As they trudged home, Heema asked, " Do you
think mother will put feathers or shells on these
new baskets? "

" I don't know," answered Docas, " but she will
make a pretty pattern with the dark fern stems
or the willow bark."

Next morning Ama began making the new
basket.   She made this basket flat.

By the time the basket was finished, the grass-
seed was ripe in the fields around them.

One morning Ama got up very early.   Docas
saw her pick up the new flat basket and a deep
basket with a handle.

" I'm going to see what she does with the new
basket," thought Docas, creeping out very softly.

"I can carry the new basket," said Docas.

He trotted along behind Ama as she walked out to the field of grass. The grass was so tall that Docas was almost hidden, and his mother did not see him.

Docas watched Ama brush the tops of the grass with the flat basket. Every few minutes there would come a little rattle as Ama knocked the seeds down into the deep basket. "Just hear the grass-seed rattle down into the deep basket," said Docas to himself.

The poppies were still asleep. Docas tried to poke some of them open, but they closed tightly again. He pulled some of the little green caps off the buds, but the little golden buds refused to open.

"They want the sun to drive away the mist before they wake up. Everything is sleepy this morning except mother. I think I'm sleepy myself." With that he fell asleep among the poppies, with the tall grasses nodding over him. After a little Ama came over that way, brushing the grass tops as she came. Suddenly she stumbled and looked down.

"Why! There's a child! It's my own little Docas!" she exclaimed.

Docas rubbed his eyes and looked at her. Then he rolled out of her way and jumped up.

By that time the basket was full of seeds, so they started back to the rancheria. Ama slung the deep basket on her back, carrying it by a strap across her forehead.

" I can carry the new basket," said Docas.

After they came to the rancheria, Ama made the grass-seed into bread for breakfast.

DOCAS'S NEW SKIRT.

MASSEA and some of the other Indian men went out to hunt deer. Docas ran to meet them as they came home.

" How many did you get? One, two, three, four, five, six," he said, counting the deer.

Then he ran to his mother and said, " Oh, mother, may I not have a new skirt? I want one of deer-skin instead of rabbit-skin this time."

" Yes, you shall have it as soon as I can make it for you," answered his mother.

After the deer were skinned, Ama took up a skin and said to Docas, " Put it into a still pool in the creek and let it stay there."

" How long must it stay? " asked Docas.

" Until the hair is loose," answered Ama.

So every morning Docas went out to the skin to see if the hair was loose. One morning he came running to his mother, crying, " Look, mother, I pulled this bunch of hair out so easily this morning! "

Then Ama took the skin out of the water.

"You may pull all the hair out," she said to Docas. "After that I will scrape it with a sharp stone."

When both sides were scraped clean, Ama and Docas went out into the woods.

"We must find two trees so close together that we can stretch the skin between them," said Ama.

By and by they found them, stretched the skin, and went back to camp. Every little while Docas went running out to the skin to see how fast it was drying.

"It just seems as if I couldn't wait for my new skirt," he said.

When it was half dry, Ama warmed some deer's brains at the fire.

"Now, Docas, get the deerskin," she said. "You may rub some brains of a deer on the skin."

Docas rubbed and rubbed for a long time.

"Haven't I rubbed enough?" he asked after a while.

"No, you must get the skin very soft," she answered.

Docas's arms grew tired after a little, so Ama said, "Go out where the ground is wet and dig a hole. I will finish rubbing the skin."

By the time the hole was ready the skin was

Massea bringing home a deer.

soft. Ama brought it to the hole and said, " Now we will bury the skin for four or five weeks."

" Bury it!" exclaimed Docas. " I thought it was ready to make into my skirt, now."

" Not yet," answered Ama.

For several days Docas kept asking Ama if the skin was not almost ready, but after a while he grew tired of asking and forgot all about it.

When the time was up, Ama went out to the hole one evening after Docas was asleep. She dug up the skin, cleaned it, and made it into a skirt. She put a fringe on the bottom of the skirt to finish it off. After the skirt was done she laid it by Docas's side, where he would see it the first thing in the morning.

Such a happy boy as he was when he found his new skirt!

THE SWEAT HOUSE.

MASSEA and the other Indian men were not feeling well one day. They said, " We ate too much deer. We must go to the sweat house."

The Indians had dug a large hole in the ground and made a rude cave. They had covered this with brush, leaving only one little hole for a door. They called this place the sweat house.

" Look at them! There they go!" cried Docas to Heema

As the Indians went into the sweat house, Massea said to Docas : —

" Build a fire in the doorway so that we cannot get out."

The sweat house was almost full of Indians, and after the fire was built they began to dance. They danced as hard as they could.

" I should not like to be in there," said Docas to Heema. " Just think how hot it must be ! "

" Hear them grunt ! " exclaimed Heema.

It grew hotter and hotter in the sweat house, but the men kept on dancing.

Soon the sweat began to pour off them until the ground was wet. Massea went around with a scraper and scraped the other Indians.

By and by the fire went down, and Docas went off to play. By that time the Indians were tired out.

" Look at them ! There they go ! " cried Docas to Heema. Massea and the other men had jumped over the fire at the door and were running down to the river.

Heema and Alachu came running.

" Now father's in the water ! " cried Docas. A moment later he added, " See, he has come up out of the river. They are going to lie down in the sun to get warm and dry again. Let's go down and play in the sun near them."

THE FEAST OF THE EAGLES.

IN the mountains near the camp was a gorge where the eagles built their nests. One day, Massea said to the other men:—

"To-morrow we will get the eagles."

Next morning early they started.

"We shall not be back until evening," said Massea to Docas. "The eagles build their nests so high among the rocks that it is hard to reach them."

It was so late before the men came back that Docas was asleep, but he waked when he heard the voices. He looked out of the hut; then he shook Heema, saying, "Wake up, Heema; father has brought home two little eagles."

"Let me take them to their huts," said Docas to his father.

Docas took the little eagles and put them into two brush huts that had been built for them.

Little Umwa had died a few weeks before, so every day Massea, Ama, and the children went to see the eagles. Docas always took them something to eat.

"Tell Umwa we love her still," said Docas to the eagles.

"Tell Umwa I'll take good care of her if she will come back," said Heema.

" Tell Umwa 'Lachu want to play," said little Alachu.

The father and mother also told the eagles many things to tell their baby, for the Indians thought that the eagles would see Umwa, and could talk to her after they were killed.

The men built a very large brush hut, large enough to hold all the Indians in the village. At the end of two weeks, Massea said, " Now we will build a fire in the big hut."

As the sun set they began dancing around the fire, and danced all night until almost sunrise. Each carried in his hands a bunch of owl feathers tied to a stick, with rattles from a rattlesnake in among the feathers. Whenever the bunch was shaken it made a rattling noise.

Several times during the night Massea threw baskets on the fire. Sometimes the baskets rolled off without burning. Massea put those baskets into the laps of women who were sitting near the fire, saying to them, " Give these baskets to the poor people."

This went on till sunrise, and then the fire was made to burn very brightly. The eagles were killed and their bodies were laid on the fire. As the bodies burned, Massea danced more wildly than ever, shaking the rattle even more rapidly. And all the time he kept calling, " Don't forget to tell Umwa."

" Tell Umwa we love her still."

THE INVITATION TO THE DANCE.

ONE day Docas and his little brother Heema were playing near their brush hut, when Docas heard a slight noise near by. He looked up and saw another Indian boy about twelve years old. The boy held in his hand some strings of deerskin.

"It's Apa, whose father is chief of the camp nearest us," Docas said.

The boy Apa came forward. "Where's your father?" he asked.

"In the sweat house," answered Docas.

"Give him this string when he comes out," said Apa, taking one of the strings from the little bunch. "Good-by. I have more camps to visit to-day," and he started off on the run.

Docas and Heema looked the string over as soon as Apa had gone. They found five knots tied in it, each a little way apart from the others.

"I wonder what the knots are for," said Heema. "Do they mean that they wish to fight us?"

"No, for Apa's father is our friend. Here comes father. We will ask him," answered Docas.

Docas and Heema ran toward Massea and gave him the string. As they passed Ama she saw the string and smiled. When they gave it to Massea, he smiled, too, and said, "It is well."

"What does it mean, father?" asked Heema. "Why do you and mother smile when you see it?"

"It means that Chief Yeeta sends to Chief Massea an invitation for everybody in our rancheria to come to a dance at his rancheria," answered Massea.

"All right. Let's go this morning," said Heema, starting toward the hut to get the new rabbit-skin skirt his mother had just made for him.

"Wait," said Massea. "The five knots mean that we are not to come for five days."

"Oh, that's so long to wait," said Heema.

"You can watch the time for us," said Massea. "Every morning you may untie one of the knots for us, and when the last but one is reached, we will start."

So every morning, as soon as it was light, the two boys crept out of the hut and untied a knot.

THE ACORN DANCE.

"THERE'S only one knot left. Can't we start now?" shouted Heema, as he untied the next to the last knot.

"Not until afternoon; but you may go to the marsh with me to gather reeds to blow on at the dance," answered Massea.

Just before lunch, Heema burst into the hut,

where Ama was busy putting food into their baskets.

"I got all these reeds myself and I tied them together myself," he cried. He held up a bunch of reeds tied together with a deerskin string and almost as big as he was.

"Such fun as we shall have at the acorn dance!" he exclaimed, pulling a reed out of the bunch, and cutting it in such a manner that it made a rude flute. He began to jump around the hut, blowing on the reed meanwhile. As he gave an extra big jump, he lit on the edge of one of the baskets, tipped it over, and spilled the clams in it all over the ground.

"I wish you would be more quiet, like Docas," said Ama.

"Never mind, I'll pick up the clams," said Heema, hurrying to get the clams back into the basket again. "Docas wants to be a man. You can't have much fun with him these days," he said.

Just as he put the last clam back, Docas and Massea came in sight, and Heema ran to meet them.

By the middle of the afternoon, everything was ready, and they started with their reeds for the village of Chief Yeeta. They carried a great many clams and much grass-seed bread, for they were to be gone several days. Yeeta's village

The Red Deer.

was about eight miles away, by the side of a little brook.

Docas walked quietly along by Massea's side, but Heema ran around so much, chasing squirrels, that he began to grow tired.

Suddenly Docas said, " There's Apa."

" He has come to meet us. We must be almost there," said Heema, forgetting that he was tired, and running forward.

From the top of the next hill Heema could look down on the village where Apa lived. In a minute he came running back to Docas.

" Oh, there are so many people there! And they are making a big circle by sticking green boughs in the ground out in an open place," exclaimed Heema. " Please hurry up, Docas, you are so slow."

Docas laughed and said, " Not when I get started, Heema," and he began running toward Apa. Docas could run fast, so he reached Apa long before Heema did.

" Why are the people putting grass down in a circle? " asked Heema, as the three boys walked into the village.

" That's where they dance, and they want it to be soft so that they can lie down when they get tired," answered Docas.

It was dark before all the invited people had come, so they all had supper and went to bed.

Next morning the dancing began. Massea stood on one side and stamped on a hollow log, while the women and the other men made one big circle, and swayed back and forth, singing as they danced. They kept time with their singing and dancing to Massea's stamping.

By and by they grew tired and stopped dancing.

Heema had gone down to the brook, for he was tired of watching the dance.

"Come, Heema," called Docas. "We must take around the acorn porridge now. The people are hungry."

After the porridge had been served, the men stepped out again into the circle, while the women sat on the ground outside and looked on. Yeeta had a big rattle in his hand, and each of the other men had a reed.

Yeeta stood in the centre and shook his rattle. The other men blew on their reeds, and began jumping toward the right. The dance went on for a little while, and then suddenly Yeeta stopped shaking the rattle. The men, who were watching him, stopped dancing and blowing their reeds at the same time.

"Good," said Docas, who was standing near. "No one got caught that time."

Yeeta again began shaking his rattle, and the dance went on once more. This time he had been shaking the rattle for a long while, when suddenly he stopped a second time.

"Look at them! Look at them! Half the men were not looking at him, and they are still dancing," shouted Docas, and he laughed and pointed his finger at the dancers who were caught. The other boys laughed too, and the careless men looked foolish.

And so the dance went on for days, until they had eaten all the food they had with them. As they went home, Docas said to Heema, "I wish next autumn were here so that the acorns would be ripe again, and it would be time for another acorn dance."

DOCAS PLAYING "TEEKEL."

"OH, Docas, I am so tired of working! Let's play something," said Heema one evening.

"Help me get the boys together and we will play teekel. Father and the other men played it last night," answered Docas.

Docas and Heema ran through the rancheria shouting, "Come play teekel! Come play teekel!" as loud as they could.

Before five minutes had passed, a crowd of boys were gathered in an open space at one side of the rancheria. Each boy brought with him a long, slender stick about as tall as himself.

" I will get the ball, if you will make the lines,"
shouted Docas, running toward the hut.

In a minute Docas came back carrying the ball,
which was made of deerskin and looked like a
small dumb-bell. While he was gone, the boys
had scratched two long lines in the ground about
ten feet apart. The lines were in the middle of
the open space.

" You haven't made the hole for the ball yet,"
said Docas. He dug out a little hole midway
between the two lines and laid the ball in it.

" We'll give you first hit, and then we'll get the
ball back over your goal," said Heema, tossing
the ball up into the air for Docas to strike at
with his stick.

But Docas hit the ball and sent it flying toward
Heema's goal.

" After it, boys!" shouted Heema.

In an instant the whole mass of boys were
rushing toward the ball. Then such a running
to and fro as there was! Back and forth went
the ball, first toward one goal, then toward the
other.

Such wild blows as were aimed at the ball!
Sometimes they hit it, but more often the sticks ·
beat the air wildly, or else fell on some boy's head
or shoulders. Not a boy cried even if the blows
did hurt, because, they thought, " Our fathers did
not cry when they played last night, and we must

not be less brave." But they shouted and laughed so much that Massea came out to see what was going on.

"Run, Docas, run!" shouted Massea, as one of the boys on Docas's side sent the ball flying far over the heads of the other boys, and down toward where Docas was standing near his goal.

And Docas did run. He knew that the boys on the other side were coming as fast as they could. He knew that he was the only boy on his side who was near the ball, and that unless he reached it first they would send it back over to their goal. He knew that Massea and the other men were watching him.

On came the crowd of boys. Now they were so near that their sticks were raised to strike the ball back. But Docas slipped in just ahead, hit the ball and sent it flying over his goal. Docas had fallen, but the other boys could not stop. They tumbled over Docas, and then in an instant there was a mixture of boys and sticks in a heap on the ground, with Docas at the bottom.

In a minute more, however, they were on their feet. Docas got up and laughed, although he had a big lump on his forehead. He was happy, for he had won the game. And more than that, Massea's hand lay on his head for an instant, as he said, " My oldest son. He will be a man like his father some day."

And sent it flying over his goal.

MAKING THE MOUNTAINS.

ONE summer Massea went across the mountains east of the rancheria to the big valley beyond. He went to make a visit and to get some good wood from which to make bows, for the best wood for bows grew only on the mountains which were farther to the east.

When he came back, all the Indians were lying around the campfire after supper.

" Tell us what you saw, father," said Docas.

" I saw great mountains beyond the big valley."

" Bigger mountains than ours ? " asked Docas.

" Yes, mountains so high that it is always winter on their tops," answered Massea.

" I don't see how the mountains ever came to be so big," said Heema.

" Shall I tell you a story about how the mountains were made ? I heard one over there," said Massea.

" Yes ! Yes ! " cried the children.

" Once upon a time there was nothing in the world but water. Where Tulare Lake now is, there was a pole standing up out of the water, and on it sat a hawk and a crow. First one of them would sit on it awhile, then the other would take his turn. Thus they sat on the pole above the water for a long, long time."

" How long ? " asked Docas.

" A great many times as long as you are years old," answered Massea. " At last they grew tired of living all alone, so they made some birds. They made the birds that live on fish, such as the king-fisher, the duck, and the eagle. Among them was a very small duck. This duck dived down to the bottom of the water and came up with its beak full of mud. When it came to the top it died; then it lay floating on the water.

" The hawk and the crow then gathered the mud from the duck's mouth."

" What did they do with it ? " asked Alachu.

" Keep still, Alachu, and let father tell the story," said Docas.

" They began to make the mountains. They began away south. We call the place Tehachapi Pass now. The hawk made the eastern range, and the crow made the western. Little by little, as they dropped in bit after bit of the earth, the mountains grew. By and by they rose above the water. Finally the hawk and the crow met in the north at Mount Shasta. When they compared their mountains, the eastern range was much smaller than the western.

" Then the hawk said to the crow, ' You have played a joke on me. You have taken some of the earth out of my bill. That is why your moun-tains are larger.'.

" It was so, and the crow laughed in his claws. The hawk did not know what to do, but at last he got an Indian weed and chewed it. This weed made him very wise, so he took hold of the mountains and slipped them round in a circle. He put the range he had made in place of the other. That is why the mountains east of the big valley are now larger than our Coast Range."

THE MEASURING-WORM ROCK.

WHEN Massea had finished his story, Docas said, " Tell us another, father!"

" Yes, tell us another ! " cried all the children.

By this time every child in the rancheria had come to listen.

" Very well," said Massea. " When I was over in the great mountains, I saw a valley, the Yosemite, with one rocky wall going up out of it a mile high. The Indians over there told me a story about that rock. There were once two little boys living in a valley. These boys went down to the river to swim, and after they had paddled about awhile, one said, ' I am going on shore to take a sleep.'

" ' I am going with you. We will lie down in the sun on that rock,' said the second boy.

" They both lay down on the rock and fell fast asleep. They slept so long that winter came and then the next summer. Another summer and winter came, and still they slept on. Summer after summer went by, and still the children did not wake.

" Meanwhile the rock on which they lay was rising slowly into the air. Day after day, and night after night, it rose higher and higher, until soon they were up beyond the reach of their friends. Far up, far up they went until their faces scraped the moon, and still the children slept.

" At length all the animals came together, for they intended to get the boys down in some way.

" ' Suppose we all make a spring up the wall. Some of us will be sure to reach the top,' said the lion.

" ' Agreed,' said the others.

" One by one they began to jump. The little mouse jumped up a hand-breadth. The rat jumped two hand-breadths. The raccoon jumped a little higher; and so on.

" All the smaller animals had failed when the grizzly bear came to take his turn.

" ' I shall jump far higher than any of you. I shall get to the top,' said the bear.

" He gave a tremendous leap, but he, too, failed.

" Last of all came the lion. ' It is not strange that you have all failed. You are not lions. But I am the king of beasts. I shall bring the little boys down,' said he.

"He stepped back from the wall, then he ran and jumped with all his might. He jumped higher than any of the others, but the top of the rock was still far above him, so he fell back and tumbled flat on his back.

"Without saying anything, a tiny little measuring-worm began to creep up the rock. It was so tiny that none of the animals noticed it. Little by little, it crept slowly upward. Presently it was above the bear's jump, then it was far above the lion's jump, then it was out of sight."

"Please hurry up, father," said Alachu. "I can scarcely wait to see if it got the little boys."

Massea only smiled and went on. "So it crawled up, and up, and up, through many winters, and at last it reached the top."

"Goody!" cried Alachu, clapping her hands. "Then what did it do?"

"Then the measuring-worm took the little boys and brought them down the way it went up."

THE FIRST WHITE MAN.

ONE morning Massea said, "I am going out to hunt deer to-day."

Docas went to a corner of the cave and got a deer's head with the horns on it, and gave it to Massea. Massea took the head, picked up his bow and arrows, and went away. He carried it until he had walked nearly to the top of the mountains, then he tied the deer's head on top of his own head.

After that he looked as if he were a deer himself as he walked along through the bushes. He did this so that he would not frighten any deer which might see him coming.

By and by he saw some deer not very far off. He bent down so that only his horns showed above the bushes; then he walked toward the deer. They looked up when they heard the noise, and saw the deer's head coming toward them. "It's nothing but another deer," they thought.

Massea kept walking closer and closer to them until he was so near that he was sure he could hit them. Then he raised his bow, put the arrow into its place, pulled the string, and took good aim. He let go the string, and the arrow flew. In a minute more a large deer was lying dead, and the others were running away.

Massea went up to the dead deer. When he saw how large it was he said to himself, "That will give Ama and Docas something to eat for a long time." He threw the deer over his shoulder and started to carry it home.

After a while he became tired, so he lay down to rest under a big redwood tree. By and by he

heard a noise and looked up, and there, a little
way off, were three deer. He picked up his
bow and arrows to shoot, but saw something
that surprised him so much that he stopped.

He saw two·men with white·skins. They did
not see Massea, because they too were looking at
the deer. One of them raised something long
and black which he had in his hand. There was
a loud noise, and one of the deer·fell dead.

Massea was frightened, for he had never seen
white men before. He hid himself so that they
could not see him. He was afraid they might
kill him in the same way that they had killed
the deer, without even using a bow and arrow.

They picked up their deer and went off toward
the ocean. Massea followed a little way behind
until he saw that they were going down the
mountains. Then he came back to where he had
left his deer, and carried it down to the Indian
rancheria. You can imagine how surprised the
Indians were when he told them what he had
seen.

A few days later, Docas and some of the other
Indian boys were playing at the edge of the camp,
when Docas heard a noise and looked up.

"Look! What's that queer animal coming
toward us?" he said.

"It has two heads!" exclaimed Heema.

The children were so surprised that they did

"That will give Ama and Docas something to eat for a long time."

not think of running. They just sat still and looked at this thing as it came nearer.

"There are three more of them," cried Docas. "They are coming toward us, too."

"Now the first one is stopping! Now it's breaking in two!" exclaimed Heema.

In a moment more, however, the children found that it was not one creature. It was a white man riding on a queer little animal with long ears that wagged backward and forward.

They walked toward Docas, and Docas called his father. Massea did not run away, but came up to where they were. The white men told Massea by signs that they were trying to find out how far the great bay extended to the south.

Massea showed them as well as he could. The white men made the Indians understand that they were going round the bay, and that there were more white men camped on a creek a few miles back.

After they had gone on, a great many of the Indians went up to the camp to see the white men. They took them some acorn meal to eat.

At the camp they found the white chief, Governor Portola. The white men had more of the strange animals at the camp. They let Docas and his little brother Heema look at them as long as they liked. Heema said to Docas, "Oh,

Docas, do you think they would let me ride one of the queer animals a little way ? "

Docas said, " I don't know, but I will ask and find out."

The white men smiled and nodded when they understood what Docas wanted. Docas went to Heema and said, " They do not care."

In a moment Heema was seated on the mule's back. As the mule began to walk, Heema held very tightly to the saddle.

" Riding a mule is easy," said Heema.

" Let me try," said Docas.

Docas led the mule to a rock, and Heema jumped down. Docas rode around until Massea said, " It is time to go home."

After a day or two, the men who had gone south around the bay came back, then the whole party went away over the mountains to the ocean again. That was the last that Docas saw of the white men for eight years.

DOCAS GOES TO THE RED HILL.

ONE day Massea said, " Docas, we have used the last of our red earth. We must go to the red hill and get some more." They wanted the red earth to paint their bodies.

Next morning they started very early, while it was still cold. They went to the creek near by and took some mud from the bank.   This they smeared all over their bodies to keep them warm. After they were covered with mud the cold wind did not strike the bare skin, so they were warmer.

Then they walked south across the valley toward what we now call the New Almaden Mine.   Docas was old enough and strong enough to walk almost as far as his father.

A little after noon they came to the hill where the red earth was.   They filled some baskets with it and sat down to rest.   They soon saw five more Indians coming with empty baskets.

When they came nearer Massea spoke to them, and asked them from what place they came.   They said they lived over on the coast on the southern part of the big bay.   They told Massea that they had gone to live at what was called the Carmel Mission.   Massea had never heard of a mission before, so he asked them to tell him what it was.

One of the strange Indians said, " Some white men came and settled near our rancheria."

Docas had been sitting by his father's side all this time, listening.   When he heard this, he said to Massea, " Oh, father, perhaps it is some of the white men who came past our rancheria when I was a little boy."

Massea said, " Perhaps."

Then he asked the strange Indian if they were

the white men who had come across the moun·
tains about eight summers ago.

The Indian said, " No; but they were friends."

He then said to Massea and Docas, " We call
the white men 'father.' They are very good to
us. They showed us how to make a very large
house. It is not made of brush, but is made of
clay, and we call this house the church."

" How big is it?" asked Docas.

" It is so large that many oak trees could stand
inside it. On the walls are things that, when
you come in front of them, show your face clearer
than the quietest spring of water. Then there
are long white sticks that make a soft light when
they are lit. But the most beautiful things in
the church are the pictures."

" What are pictures?" asked Massea.

" Flat things that hang on the wall and look
like people," the stranger answered.

He stopped for a while after he had told all
this. Massea and Docas did not say anything.
By and by he said, " The fathers have been kind
to us, so I have gone to live with them. I am a
Mission Indian now." After this Massea and
Docas asked him many questions about how
they lived.

Before he went away, Massea said to him, " I
think I should like to be a Mission Indian. Are
not any of the fathers coming over across the
mountains?"

The strange Indian from Monterey said, " Yes, a little while ago a new father, called Father Pena, came to our Mission.   He soon started over the mountains to begin a new Mission.   He must be out in the valley somewhere now."

After a while, Massea and Docas took up their baskets and started off.   All the way home they kept talking about the Mission and what the Indian from Monterey had told. them.

That night, as they sat around the campfire, Massea told the other Indians all they had heard that day.   Some of the Indians laughed at the story, but Massea said, " If one of the fathers comes over here, I am going to know more about him.   Perhaps I shall go to live with him."

DOCAS IN A FIGHT.

A FEW days after this visit to the red hill, Massea and his family saw some white men coming into the rancheria.   Three of them were riding on animals very much like those ridden by Portola's men; but these were not mules — they were horses.

Each man wore a cloak of padded deerskin. Arrows could not go through these cloaks, so the white men always wore them.   Sometimes the Indians shot arrows at them, but when they came to this rancheria the Indians did not try to hurt them. They gave the white men some acorn mush to eat.

While they were eating, Docas crept up to his father and said, " Do you think that man with the long dark dress is the father the Indian from the coast told about ? "

Massea said, " I think so, but we will see after dinner."

The white men had an Indian with them who could talk both Indian and Spanish. After they had eaten, they began to talk to the Indians.

Docas was right. One of the men was Father Pena, who had come into their valley to start a new mission.

He went about ten miles farther south. There he started the new mission, and called it Santa Clara, after a very good and beautiful woman.

One day, a few weeks later, Massea got into a quarrel with some Indians from another rancheria, about some deer they had trapped. That night Docas heard something go "thud" by the side of his head while he was asleep. He put out his hand and felt an arrow sticking in the ground beside the tule mat on which he was sleeping.

" Some one is shooting at us," he shouted.

Massea jumped up and got his own bow and arrows. He came over and felt of the arrow that had been shot into the hut, to see from what direc-tion it came.

Massea gave a long call to tell the Indians of their rancheria that there was danger and that they must help. Then he and Docas crept out of the house and hid behind two trees that stood near the front of the hut. In a moment more they saw some dark figures moving about in the direction from which the arrow had come.

They raised their bows and were just going to shoot, when they heard a rustle behind them. They turned quickly, but before they could help themselves, their arms were seized and tied behind their backs.

" Now we have you," said the strange Indians.

Some of the strange Indians hurried into the hut and brought out Ama, Heema, and Alachu and took them off. The others stayed to fight.

Next day they took Massea and his family out to the middle of their rancheria. The Indians who had captured them were going to torture them.

Suddenly a man in a long gray gown stood among them. It was Father Pena, and he was holding up a cross.

He said, " My children, what are you doing ? Do you know that it is wrong for you to torture your neighbors ? Let them go."

These Indians loved Father Pena already and wanted to do as he told them, so they let Massea go, and all his family with him.

PART II.

WHEN DOCAS LIVED AT THE MISSION.

He decided to go to the Mission to live.

PART II.

DOCAS GOES TO LIVE AT THE MISSION.

AFTER Father Pena had saved Massea from being tortured, Massea liked him very much, —so much that he decided to go to the Mission to live.

Therefore after a few days they gathered together their baskets, their bows and arrows, and some seeds. Then they were ready to start, for they had nothing more to take with them. Docas walked with Heema, his little brother. Massea walked at the side of Ama, who was carrying Keoka, Docas's baby sister. Alachu trotted behind.

When they came to the Mission they found that some of the Indians who were already there had helped Father Pena to build a very large brush house. This the Father called a church. Near it was the Father's hut, and off at one side were the huts of the Indians. These huts were built in rows, but they were of brush just as they had always been.

As soon as they arrived, Docas and Massea went off a little way to the creek, where there were many willow trees growing. They broke off the leafy branches and carried them up to the Mission to make their own hut. When they had a large pile of branches they began to build it.

First they stuck one end of a branch into the ground. They did that with all the branches until they had a circle, putting the branches so close together that Docas could hardly look between them.

When the circle was finished, they bent all the tops of the branches together and tied them; then they covered the house with dry grass.

The Father tried to get Massea to build a better kind of house; he said he would show him how to do it, for the brush house was too cold. But Massea said, " No; we like this kind of house. When it gets too dirty, we will burn it down and build another."

They left a little hole for a door. They left it open all the time because they had nothing with which to close it.

After the house was finished and the baskets were put away in it, they all went to help their friends build their houses. One of the Indians who was already living at the Mission brought them a bundle of straw, which Massea put across the hole in front of their house. That meant to any Indian who might come to see them, " We are away from home, and shall be gone some time."

BREAKFAST AT THE MISSION.

NEXT morning Ama got up very early. She went down to the creek bed and hunted about until she found two stones that she liked. One was large and flat on top; the other was small and long, with one end that had been worn smooth by the water. She wanted to make a new mortar and pestle, for the old ones were so heavy that she had not brought them with her.

Ama carried her corn down to the creek, put it on the big stone, and tried to pound it with the little one; but the corn flew all over the ground, for there was no hole worn yet in the top of the flat rock.

She poured some more corn on the top of the flat stone, but this time she did not pound it so hard. Even then she could not grind it very well, but by and by it was fine enough so that she could make mush of it.

She started to go to the hut to tell Docas to make a fire. Just as she climbed up the bank the sun came over the top of the mountain. It shone on the queer, shiny thing that looked something like a basket upside down. This thing hung between two posts by the church, and it was shining so brightly now that Ama could hardly look at it.

At the same moment that the sun rose, she heard something go, "Clang, clang, clang!" The sound seemed to come from this same shiny thing.

It waked Massea and Docas, and they came running out of the hut to see what was the matter. In a few minutes all the other people in the village came out of their huts, too.

Everybody seemed to be going toward the shiny thing that made the noise. So Ama snatched up little Keoka, and they all followed after the other people to see what was the matter.

They found that all the Indians were going into the big brush house, and they followed. As the people went in they knelt down. Massea said, "I am going to do as other people do," so he knelt down, too. Then he took Ama and the children and went to a corner of the house to see what was going to happen.

Up in the front of the house some of the long white sticks were burning that the Indian from Monterey had told about. In a few minutes more Docas heard the sweetest sound! Heema began to talk to him just then, but Docas said, "Stop! I want to listen."

In a few minutes some more boys came in, all

singing. Docas could not understand anything they said, but he liked the sound.

Then Father Pena came out and said some·thing, but Docas could not understand that either. After the little boys had sung, everybody got up and went out of the house. Massea and his family followed, and they all went back to their homes.

Ama asked Docas to build the fire. He found some dry sticks and soon had a fire roaring. Just then a strange little Mission boy with a red skirt on came up. "What are you building that fire for?" he said.

"For my mother to cook breakfast," answered Docas.

"We don't do that here at the Mission," said the strange Indian boy.

"Don't have any breakfast?" asked Docas. Docas was almost ready to wish he were back at the old rancheria, if he could not have any breakfast.

"Oh, no!" said the boy. "I meant that each family does not get its own breakfast."

"Then who does get it?" asked Docas.

"Well, you see my mother and some of the other women stayed home and got breakfast ready for all of us while we were at mass," said the boy. Then he asked, "Where is your mother?"

"She is down at the creek trying to grind some more corn while I build the fire," answered Docas.

"Let's surprise her," said the boy. "Have you some baskets? Get one, and we will go and get the breakfast while she is gone."

Docas went into the hut and brought out one of the flat baskets. The boy looked at it; then he said, "Haven't you any deeper basket? They give you so much to eat here." Docas went back, and this time he brought out one of the deep baskets in which Ama used to carry the grass-seed. Then they went off.

Soon Ama came back. She looked all round, but could not find any fire. "I wonder what has become of Docas," she said.

Docas had not put any big wood on the fire, but only some small sticks, so by the time Ama came up from the creek it was all burned out.

In a little while Ama saw Docas coming toward them, carrying a basket very carefully in his hands. The other Indian boy was with him.

"I wonder where he has been and what he is carrying in that basket. I should think he would be hungry himself, and build the fire, instead of running off to play before breakfast," thought Ama.

In a minute more Docas set the basket down at her feet. She looked into it, then she said.

"Why, it is filled with mush. Where did you get it?"

Docas then told Ama about the big boilers full of mush, and how every family sent and got its breakfast from them.

The strange little boy, whose name was Yisoo, said, "Good-by; I will be back after breakfast, but I must hurry now and take our breakfast home."

✝

THE MISSION SCHOOL.

AFTER a little while Yisoo came back. "Come now; it is time to go to school," said he.

"What is school? What do you do there?" asked Docas.

"Why, it's a place where all the Indian boys go every day. They just say over things that the Father tells them."

"Is that all? I don't think that's any fun," said Docas.

"No, it isn't," said the boy; "but I tell you what is fun," he added. "If you have a good voice, the Father will teach you to sing and maybe he will teach you to play on a violin."

Docas was glad to hear that perhaps he could learn to sing, for he loved music. As they walked along Yisoo told Docas about what he must do at school.

As they came out of the school, Yisoo said to Docas, "I can beat you home." They both started off on a run, but Docas came out a little ahead. Yisoo looked at his bare legs and said, "You know how to run."

Docas said, "Yes; but you see I haven't so many clothes on as you."

"I must take you after dinner to get some clothes like mine," said Yisoo.

They hurried to get their baskets and go for the dinner. For dinner they had some meat as well as mush. Father Pena told the women who were giving out the dinner that both Docas and Yisoo had studied very hard that morning, and if there were any scraps of dinner left they should have them. So Docas and Yisoo had a big dinner that day, for when they came back, the women gave them each an extra piece of meat and a little cake made of corn.

After dinner, Yisoo said, "Now we will go for your clothes."

They went to the house where the Indian clothes were kept. Father Pena went with them and gave Docas a suit of clothes just like Yisoo's. Docas liked them very much, for the jacket was white and the shirt was scarlet.

After Docas was dressed, Father Pena said "Haven't you a brother and a sister?"

"Yes, Father," said Docas.

"Then take them each a suit of clothes, too. All the children here wear the same kind of clothes," said Father Pena.

RAISING CORN.

THE place the Fathers first selected for the Mission was very low, and before they had lived there many winters, a great rain made the creek overflow its banks and flood the Mission.

"This place is too low; we must move farther away from the creek," said the Fathers, as they watched the muddy water swirling about among their houses.

So before long the entire Mission was moved three miles away to a safe place.

Father Joseph was the name of the younger of the two Fathers. He had charge of the Mission gardens, and one day in May he walked out among the gardens that had been planted. Massea was at work pulling weeds. As Father Joseph came near, he said, "Massea, our garden needs more water."

Massea said, "Yes, it is too dry; but there will be no rain for three or four months yet."

"What can we do to bring some water to the garden?" said Father Joseph. "I wonder if we could not make a long ditch from the Guadalupe Creek around our garden and then back to the creek again."

"It would bring the water, but it would be much work, Father," said Massea.

"We have many Indians who could work," said Father Joseph. "I will ask Father Pena what he thinks about it."

Father Pena thought the idea was a good one. So in a few days, after they had marked out the course of the ditch, there were two hundred Indian men at work digging. Even Docas worked after school was done. They worked so hard that in a few weeks the ditch was made, and part of the water of the creek was flowing through it. After that the gardens were never dry any more.

The children liked the ditch too, for it was such a fine place to go wading in. Heema made tiny boats out of tules[1] as nearly like Massea's big boat as he could. Even Docas liked to watch his little brother and sister sail their boats on the water in the ditch.

By the side of the irrigating ditch grew many rows of corn. When it was ripe, Massea went to his house and got a very large, deep basket.

Docas said, "Where are you going, father?"

---

[1] *Tu'le*, a large bulrush growing abundantly on overflowed land in California and elsewhere.

Massea gathering corn.

"Father Joseph told me to get this basket and cut the corn," said Massea.

"May I go with you, father?" asked Alachu.

"Yes, if you will not get in the way," said Massea.

So Massea carried his basket to the cornfield, and Alachu trotted along by his side. He went down each row of corn, cutting off the heads and putting them into his basket. Sometimes he happened to drop a head, but when he did that, Alachu picked it up for him, and he put it into his basket.

When the basket was full, he carried it to the end of the field where Docas was waiting with a cart drawn by oxen. Massea emptied the baskets into the cart until it was full; then Docas drove the cart to a storehouse.

One rainy day in winter when they could not work outside, Father Joseph said to a number of the Indian men, "I want you to go to the storehouse to-day to husk corn."

After school Docas went to the storehouse, too, and found Massea sitting on the floor with the other men. Massea tied a few empty husks together; then he took the ears that Docas had husked. He rubbed a full ear against the husks until all the grains of corn had dropped down into the basket on the floor.

Then it was ready to be roasted.

THRESHING THE GRAIN.

ONE morning Massea took the rough wooden plough and went out to a smooth piece of ground near the Mission. He began to plough the ground in a circle, not ploughing very deep, but only loosening the top.

Heema and Alachu were wading in the irrigating ditch.

Alachu said, "See! father is making a garden."

" That's a queer place to make a garden," said Heema.

They did not pay any more attention, but went on wading.

That afternoon Docas and some other boys and men went out with Massea to make a tight fence around the circle Massea had ploughed. Docas tied the fence together with rawhide strings so that it could not come apart.

After the fence was built, Massea poured water over the top of the ground. Then the men drove a band of wild horses into the circle and closed up the gate so that they could not get out.

When the children saw the horses going into the circle, they all ran to see what was going to happen. Docas peeped through a hole in the fence. He could see the horses standing around inside, so he called Yisoo to come and peep through, too.

One horse was standing near the hole in the fence. When he heard Docas call, he pricked up his ears, ducked his head, kicked up his heels, and started off on a run. As soon as one horse began to run all the other horses began to run, too. The children clapped their hands, and the men yelled, so the horses kept on running round and round.

By the time Father Joseph told Massea to let them out, the ground was tramped as smooth and hard as cement.

Then Massea and Docas began hauling wheat from the fields in the big ox-carts, and piling it up in the middle of the circle on the hard ground. Heema had to go to school most of the time, but Alachu rode out with Docas in the empty cart, and came back on the top of the load.

One day Docas piled the cart very full. When he was ready to go, he gave Alachu a toss up on the load, but he tossed her so hard that, instead of staying on top, she slipped clear off on the other side. Docas saw her slide off and heard a thud on the ground. He ran around the back of the cart, but he could not see Alachu. He could see only a pile of grain on the ground.

" Alachu!" he called. In a moment the grain on the ground began to shake, and Alachu's head came up out of the middle of it. A big bunch had slid off with her and covered her up.

Docas was afraid she was hurt, but when she began to laugh, he picked her up, and this time he set her very carefully on top of the hay in the cart.

By and by there was a big stack of grain in the centre of the circle. Massea spread some of the grain out on the open space between the stack and the fence, and the men turned the horses in again. Again the horses ran round and round until they had tramped all the wheat out of the grain.

Massea said to Docas, " Run, Docas. Go and get the pitchforks."

Docas ran to a house near the Father's and brought back four big, wooden pitchforks. Docas gave Massea a pitchfork. He also gave Yisoo's father one; then he gave one to Yisoo, and kept one for himself.

They went inside the circle and tossed the straw over the fence. Of course the pitchforks would not lift the wheat, so it stayed on the ground. They kept on putting down new layers of grain and letting the wild horses run over it and trample the wheat out, until there was no longer any stack in the middle.

Yisoo had the wooden shovels ready, and they shovelled all the wheat into a pile in the centre of the circle. Some of it they swept into the pile with brush brooms.

"What dirty wheat! I don't want to eat any mush made of that wheat. It's all full of little pieces of ·chaff," said Alachu. She shivered as she spoke, for a cold wind was blowing.

"Don't you want to come inside the fence? It is warmer inside," said Docas. Alachu went inside and ran over to Docas, but he said, "No, you must not stay here. Go across to the other side of the circle, close to the fence."

In a moment more she saw why Docas made her go over to the other side of the circle. Docas threw a big shovelful of the grain and chaff up into the air.

The chaff was light, and the wind blew it away, but the grain fell back to the ground. The air was so full of the bits of flying chaff that Alachu could hardly see the fence where she had been standing at first.

GETTING READY TO MAKE BRICKS.

ONE morning, Father Pena came to Massea. "I received a letter yesterday saying that a ship has come to San Francisco," he said. "It has brought some pictures for the church at our Mission. I want you to go to San Francisco with an ox-cart and bring the pictures back."

Father Pena gave Massea charge of many things. Massea had been a chief at his Indian

Threshing the grain.

rancheria, and so Father Pena sent him for the pictures.

Docas went with Massea. As they rode along they passed their old rancheria, which was deserted now.

"Where have the Indians gone?" asked Docas.

"They went away across the mountains toward the rising sun," answered Massea. "They live now in the big valley down by Tulare Lake."

The next day they came to San Francisco. Docas was much interested in the big, new church that the Indians had just finished building. It was made of adobe bricks instead of brush.

They loaded the pictures into the cart and started home. As they went slowly along, Docas said, "Why don't we have a big, new church like the one here at the Mission Dolores? I hate to. put these new pictures in the old brush house."

"We are going to build one very soon. Father Pena told me so just before we started," said Massea.

The day after Massea and Docas came home from San Francisco, Father Pena came to Docas and said, "Docas, where is the best clay bank?"

Docas thought a moment. Then he answered, "At the back of Yisoo's house. Every time we try to walk across it after a rain we get stuck."

"Let's go and take a look at it," said Father Pena.

When they got there, they found Heema and Alachu making little clay mortars and pestles out of the adobe mud.

" They play here every day," said Docas.

Father Pena picked up a dry mortar that Alachu had made a few days before. It had dried very smoothly, with no cracks in it. Father Pena nodded his head. " I think this adobe will do," he said.

On the next day Father Joseph and a number of the other men came out to the adobe bank.

" Dig up a patch of adobe," said Father Joseph to Massea.

The children all stood around and watched while Massea dug.

" Now pour some water on the adobe and mix it up," said Father Joseph.

In a few minutes Massea said, " It doesn't mix easily. The adobe is in such large lumps."

" Jump in, children, and dance around in the adobe. That will break up the lumps and make the adobe into a smooth paste," said Father Joseph.

Docas, Yisoo, and a number of the other boys jumped in.

" Take hold of hands and make a ring," said Docas. " Now we will play we are having an eagle dance."

" It's great fun ! " said Yisoo.

" I'm stuck ! " cried Docas. Yisoo and the other boys ran to him and pulled him loose from the big sticky lump in which his feet had stuck.

They jumped faster and faster. " You're jumping on my toes," cried Yisoo to Docas.

Then they both laughed, for Yisoo was not hurt.

They jumped about so fast that very soon they had crushed every lump.

While the children were jumping, Massea was sitting on the ground near by, chopping tules. He carried the chopped tules to where the children were jumping.

" Stop jumping a minute while I throw these in. Then you can mix them with the adobe," said Massea.

" What are the broken tules for ? " asked Docas.

" To make the bricks stick together better," answered Massea.

While the children were mixing the tules into the adobe paste, the men were busy, carrying piles of wooden moulds out from the Father's house.

When the adobe was smooth, Father Joseph said, " Now watch me make the first brick." He filled a mould with the mixture of adobe, tule, and water. " Now help me carry the mould to a

And there was another brick.

smooth piece of ground," said Father Joseph to Docas.

The mould had a bottom that slid out. Father Pena pulled the bottom out from under it after they set it down. Then he raised the sides of the mould, and the brick was left flat on the ground.

"What a nice brick!" said Alachu. She ran forward, and before any one could stop her, she put her hand down and tried to lift the brick. It was still soft, and her fingers made marks on it.

Father Joseph said, "You will have to wait until it dries."

Docas had watched very closely. He went back to the hole and filled a mould; then he and Heema brought it out to the smooth piece of ground. They put it down near the first brick, pulled out the bottom and raised the sides just as they had seen Father Joseph do. And there was another brick.

Soon a great many Indians were at work making the bricks, and after a little while there were rows and rows of bricks drying in the sun. They were left lying flat until they were about two-thirds dry; then Docas went around and turned them up on their edges.

GETTING THE TIMBERS.

ONE day Heema jumped into the hut where Ama was sitting. " Where's Docas ? " he asked.

" Out making bricks. What do you want of him ? " answered Ama.

" We are going up into the mountains to get a big tree. Father Joseph wants him to come and help drag it down." Before Ama could answer him he was off to find Docas.

Soon Father Joseph, Docas, Heema, and a great many other Indian men and boys started off for the mountains where the redwood trees grow. They took several oxen and several chains with them. The day before, Massea and two other men had gone up to the hills to fell the trees.

About noon the party came to the place where Massea was. He had two trees cut down, ready for them. They rested and ate some dried deer meat. After that they fastened the oxen to one of the trees that Massea had cut down; then they drove back to the Mission. The log dragged along behind the oxen until it reached the Mission.

Massea had cut down two trees. There were no oxen left to drag the second tree to the Mission, so Docas helped fasten some long chains to

the log.   Then all the Indian men and boys took
hold of the chains and dragged the log down to the
Mission themselves.   It was not very hard work,
for there were almost a hundred Indians pulling.

Early the next day they began to chop at one
of the logs with their axes to make it square.
When Massea saw that one side of it was flat he
said, "Stop."   Massea and the other men tried
to roll the log over on the other side, but it did
not move at first.

"It is heavy," said one of the men.

"Yes, but we must roll it over so that we can
smooth the other side," said Massea.

They gave another big pull all together, and
the log rolled over.

At last, instead of a rough log with bark on
it, it was a smooth, square piece of timber ready
to use in building the church.

BUILDING THE CHURCH.

AFTER they had made many bricks, Father
Joseph came to Massea and Docas and said,
" We can begin to build the church now."

Alachu had been playing with some of the
broken bricks.   That night she said to Docas,
"I think you can't build a very big church."

"Why not?" asked Docas.

"It will tumble down," said Alachu.   "I built

The day before, Massea and two men had gone to the hills to fell the trees.

up a brick wall that was not any higher than I am, and it fell over while I went to get some more bricks."

"Oh, but we are going to make ours thick. Father Joseph told father to-day that we should make the walls three feet thick. Besides, we shall fasten the bricks together with mortar."

"What's mortar?" asked Alachu.

"Sticky stuff to keep the bricks together," answered Docas.

Next morning they began to build the Mission church. Day after day they worked. Massea and some of the men spread the mortar and laid the bricks, while Docas and other men and boys made more bricks.

It took so many, many bricks!

When the side walls and the end walls were made, Father Joseph told Massea to bring two of the square timbers, and set them up exactly in the center of each of the end walls. It was hard work getting them in place. Docas had to pull with all his might.

When they were putting up the timbers, Docas saw that Father Joseph had had some of the Indians make a large notch in the upper end of each. He wanted to ask what the notch was for, but he had asked so many questions since he came to live at the Mission that he thought he would wait and see.

As soon as the two posts were up, Father Joseph had the Indians lay a long tree from one to the other in order to make the ridgepole. The ridgepole lay snugly in the notch on top, so that it could not roll off. But even with the notch, Father Joseph said the ridgepole would not be steady enough. So he gave Docas some strings made of rawhide, and told him to climb up the posts.

" What for ? " asked Docas.

" To tie the ridgepole fast to the posts," answered Father Joseph.

Docas had climbed many a tree when making storehouses for acorns, so that it was easy for him to climb the posts. He sat on top of the ridgepole after he had finished tying the posts together. Alachu was watching him from below. He waved his hand to her, and she waved hers back.

" I do hope Docas won't fall," said Alachu to Heema. Docas knew that Alachu was a little frightened, so he thought, " I'll show her what a big boy like me can do." He slipped out on the pole and swung himself around on it until he was hanging by his knees. Then he pulled himself up again on top of the pole.

Alachu called out, " Do be careful, Docas ! "

" I'm all right. Don't be scared," he called back. Then he stood up carefully and started to walk along the top of the ridgepole; but the pole was round and slippery, and he slipped. He would have fallen to the ground, but he caught hold of the ridgepole with one hand. He drew himself up again. Then he crawled back to the nearest post, slid down, and climbed off the wall to the ground.

Meanwhile, some of the Indians had been making curved tiles for the roof. The tiles were made of the same adobe mud as the bricks, but were baked in fires instead of being dried by the sun.

Alachu looked up at the ridgepole, then she looked at the tiles.

"They'll not reach from the ridgepole to the wall. They will fall through," said she.

"Not when we get ready to put them on," said Docas.

Massea had brought down from the mountains a great many smaller trees. The Indians pulled the bark from these, and laid them in rows from the ridgepole to the outer wall. Across these Massea and Docas wove a network of twigs just as they did when they made the storehouse. They tied all these trees tightly to the ridgepole so that nothing could slip.

"There," said Docas to Alachu, "do you think the tiles will fall through now when we lay them on top of that?"

So, after much work, the big church was built. The floor was covered with large, square bricks, the pictures were hung, the candles were put up. The images of the saints were placed around the walls. Near the front was a beautiful banner on which was a picture of the Mother of Jesus.

Docas was happy, for he was no longer afraid that their lovely things would get spoiled by the rain.

VISIT OF FATHER SERRA.

BY the time the church was built, Docas could sing very well. One day Father Pena gave him a new hymn to learn.

"It is very hard, Father," said Docas.

"Yes, but it is very beautiful, and I want you to be able to sing it when Father Junipero Serra visits us," said Father Pena.

"I would do anything for Father Serra," answered Docas. "He loves us so."

So every day after that for several weeks Docas practised his new hymn until he knew it perfectly. Yisoo learned it also.

"Father Serra will be pleased," said Father Pena, one day when Docas had sung the hymn very well.

Sometimes, when Docas was tired of singing,

Father Pena told him stories of Father Serra.
Once he told Docas how Father Serra had
walked hundreds of miles to start the Missions.

One morning soon after they were in school,
Massea, who had been out in the fields, came
hurrying up to the schoolroom.

"Father Serra is coming!" he called out.
Father Pena dismissed the school, and went out
to meet Father Serra. They were very glad to
see each other, for they had not met for a long
time.

Father Pena took Father Serra all over the
Mission. He showed him the fields and gardens,
and the Indian village a little way from the
church.

Father Serra said, "I am pleased to see how
well you are getting started."

This was his first visit to the Mission Santa
Clara since the new church was built.

The next day was Sunday. Docas was excited,
because Father Serra was to say the mass, and he
was to sing his new hymn.

The church was full, for the white people who
had just come to live at San José, about three
miles away, had come to church, too. By this
time most of the Indians knew when to kneel
and when to make the sign of the cross, but
Massea stood in the aisle with a long stick. It
was his duty to watch the other Indians. If one

of them forgot to kneel down at the right time Massea poked him with the end of the stick.

After the mass, Father Serra preached; then Docas and Yisoo sang their hymn. After they had sung each verse, they waited for the people to sing it over after them.

When the service was over, Docas, Yisoo, and all the other Indians who had learned to play, took their violins and walked toward Father Pena's house, playing dance music all the way. Father Pena and Father Serra walked along with them.

As they reached Father Pena's house, Father Serra happened to notice Docas. He turned and said to him, "Love God, my son."

Docas answered, "Love God, Father."

Father Serra then said, "Are you not one of the two boys who sang in church?"

"Yes, Father," answered Docas.

"You have studied well; I am pleased with you," said the Father.

Father Serra stayed until next morning, and then he went to San Francisco

VISIT OF CAPTAIN VANCOUVER.

B Y and by Docas grew to be a man, and had children of his own.

One day, as he was going home to dinner, he saw some white men ride up to the Father's house. He said to them, "Welcome. I will go and speak to the Father." He called Father Pena, who came out at once and asked the men to come into the house. He told Docas to take the horses to the stable.

The strangers told the Father that they had come to California to see what new lands they could find and to trade a little. They were the officers of a ship that was anchored in the bay near the Mission at San Francisco.

The common sailors were getting more wood and water for their ship, so the officers had been given horses by the Fathers of the Mission at San Francisco and had come down to visit the Santa Clara Mission. The name of the leader was Captain Vancouver.

Father Pena and Father Diego, who had taken the place of Father Joseph, said they were glad to see them and that the next day would be a hol'day at the Mission. The Fathers told the Indians that they might have a feast then.

Docas's little boy, who was called Oshda, always

Docas lived in a 'dobe house.

went to Father Pena's house at meal time to help wait at table. Several other Indian boys went also.

Next morning, when Father Pena was eating breakfast with Captain Vancouver, Father Pena said, " Now we'll have some fun."

He called Oshda to him and told him to bring in a plate of pancakes. Oshda smiled, for he knew what was coming. He almost ran as he went to get the cakes.

Oshda brought the plate of cakes and put it down by Father Pena. Father Pena then said, " Get into line."

Quickly all the Indian boys placed themselves in a row on the other side of the room.

Father Pena took up a cake in his hand. He said something funny to Captain Vancouver. Oshda laughed, and the moment Father Pena saw Oshda open his mouth to laugh, he threw the cake into Oshda's mouth. Oshda had to stop laughing, for his mouth was full of hot pancake.

He ate it as fast as he could, and then he was ready for another one. Father Pena kept throwing the cakes to the different boys, until no more cakes were left.

Docas went to the Father's house just before breakfast. He said to Captain Vancouver, "Some of the soldiers are going to catch and kill some cattle for the feast. Would you not like to go out and watch?"

Captain Vancouver said he would, so Docas went to the stable and saddled some of the Mission horses for them, and one for himself also. They all rode together a few miles out from the Mission, where the cattle were feeding. The soldiers rode along with them.

The cattle were very large and would not let anybody come near them. Each of the soldiers had a long rope made of horsehair, with a noose at the end. He twisted one end of the line around the pommel of his saddle. The other end with the noose he swung round and round his head. This they called a lasso.

The soldiers decided which one of the cattle they would catch first, and then several of them galloped toward the animal. When they got close enough, they all threw their lassos at the same time. One of the men caught his line around the horns of the animal, another caught its hind leg, and another its fore leg.

The horses on which the soldiers were riding stopped short, and the animal was thrown to the ground, for the ropes held him tight so that he could not move. Then another man went up to him and killed him. Twenty-two of the cattle were caught and killed in this way before Docas said it was time to go home.

"We shall have a great feast to-day," said Docas.

After the feast was over, the Indians danced and played games. The visitors again came out to watch them have a play fight.

They made Massea their chief and pretended that a large bundle of straw was the enemy. Oshda and the other boys and men got their bows and arrows. They jumped and danced around the bundle of straw, swinging their arms and yelling. Massea at last gave them a sign, and the Indians all shot their arrows at the straw bundle. Then they yelled louder than ever, for they were pretending that they had beaten the enemy.

Some of them put Massea on their shoulders, and others danced around him. They carried him up in front of the Fathers and the visitors who were watching; then they carried him back to the Indian village.

When it was time for evening service they stopped their games until after service and supper were over. In the evening they had a dance. After the visitors had stayed a day or two longer, they rode back to San Francisco.

PREPARING HIDES AND TALLOW.

A S Oshda grew older, he learned to throw the lasso. By the time he was grown he could lasso almost any of the cattle, no matter how fast his horse or the cattle were going.

He took the skin off every animal he killed and cut holes around the edge. Then he put stakes through the holes, drove the stakes into the ground as far apart as the skin would stretch, and left the skin to dry. Sometimes there were large places in the hills near the Mission, where the skins were laid so close together you could not see the ground.

Every time Oshda killed one of the cattle, he built a fire, hung some big iron kettles over it, and threw the fat parts of the cattle into these. Soon the kettles were full of boiling grease.

Docas had two more children besides Oshda, — a boy named Pantu and a little girl named Colla. Pantu and Colla liked to go with Oshda when he melted the fat. Oshda always said, though, that if they went with him they must work. There were many things they could do to help. They could bring wood and build the fire, and they could keep it going after it was built.

When the fire was built, and the fat meat was sizzling in the kettles, Oshda went off a little way

Oshda.

and dug a hole in the black adobe. Then he said to Pantu, " Run and get me some clay from the clay bank." The clay was wet and sticky. When Pantu brought it, it stuck to his fingers until his hands looked as if he had been making bricks.

Oshda took the clay and plastered the sides and bottom of the hole he had dug, smoothing them off until they were shiny. Docas came up just then with some long sticks.

Docas stuck one of the sticks in the middle of the hole.

Oshda then said to the children, " Make some more holes just like this one and stick the rest of the sticks up in them."

After the fire had burned for a long time and the grease was cooked out of the fat meat, Oshda and Docas took one of the kettles off the fire. They brought it over by the edge of the first hole and tipped it on its side. Pantu and Colla wanted to see what was going on, so they crowded up close.

" Look out! The grease is very hot. It will burn you if you are not careful," said Docas. So Pantu and Colla stepped back.

Then Docas and Oshda began to pour the hot grease into the hole. They poured until the hole was full; then they carried the kettle on to the next hole.

"What are you pouring the grease out on the ground for?" asked Pantu.

"So that it may get hard and we shall have a cake of tallow to sell," answered Docas.

Next morning Pantu and Colla woke up very early. As soon as breakfast was over, they ran out to look at the grease in the holes. Pantu could run faster than Colla, so he got there first.

"Somebody has taken out the grease and put in some white stuff," he said.

Colla took up a long stick. She stood off a little way and poked the white stuff with one end of the stick.

"It doesn't move. It's hard," she said. She poked harder, but still nothing happened. Then Colla went close to the hole, stretched out her arm, and touched the white stuff with the tip of her finger. "It feels greasy anyway, if it doesn't look like grease," said she.

Pantu came up also and touched it. "It's cold, too. Perhaps it is the grease and the cold has made it like this. You know Oshda said the grease would harden," he said.

After a little, Docas and Oshda came along.

"Come, see how hard our grease is," said Pantu.

"Yes, it is ready to put into the cart," said Oshda.

Oshda took hold of the upper end of the stick and gave a big pull. The cake of tallow came

Then Colla went close to the hole.

out of the hole with a jerk. Docas took hold of the other end of the stick on the other side of the cake of tallow, and between them they carried it away to the cart.

MAKING THE OX-CART.

ONCE Father Catala came out where Docas and Oshda were working. They were gathering up some hides and doubling them up with the hair inside. Father Catala was in charge of the Mission now, for Father Pena was dead.

Father Catala said to Docas, "We must get our hides and tallow over to Monterey. We want them to be ready for the next ship that comes to the coast to trade. Will you not begin to haul them within the next few days?"

"Yes, Father," said Docas. "But the cart I have been using has such a big axle hole in the wheel that I can hardly use it. The axle has worn the hole very large."

"Make some new wheels, and take some of the men and begin hauling the hides. We must have them down there by the time the ship comes."

Docas told Oshda to make the wheels, so Oshda went back to his house and got an axe. He lived in an adobe house now. It had two rooms below and a garret above, and a garden fenced in behind where he kept chickens.

" Where are you going and what are you going to do?" asked Pantu, his little brother.

" I am going to cut down an oak tree to make some new wheels for the cart. Do you want to come along?"

Of course Pantu wanted to come along, and he was soon skipping by Oshda's side. Oshda took such long steps that Pantu had to run part of the time to keep up with him.

They had to walk quite a distance from the Mission before they found a tree that they liked. It was about two feet through.

Oshda began chopping at the tree, while Pantu played about among the trees near by. Pantu played that he was a woodpecker and pecked away at the trunks of the trees. After he had pecked awhile, he stooped down, picked up an acorn, and stuck it into a little crack in the back of the oak tree. He pressed it in hard, so that it had to stick. So he ran from tree to tree.

After a while Oshda had chopped his tree almost through. At last the tree began to tremble and crack. He stepped back to see which way it was going.

As he did so he saw Pantu make a sudden dart across where the tree was going to fall. Pantu was not looking where he was going.

" Look out, Pantu!" Oshda called.

Pantu looked up and saw the tree falling

toward him, so he started to run faster, but it was too late. The tree came down on top of him, knocking him to the ground. He was far enough from where the tree grew so that the trunk did not fall on him. But one of the branches hit him on the head and knocked him down, while another scratched the skin off his knee.

He jumped up as soon as he could, for he knew Oshda would be frightened. Even when he was standing up, Oshda could not see him because the tree had so many branches on it, so he had to climb out from among the leaves and broken twigs. His head ached and he felt like crying, but he knew that Indian boys never cry.

When Oshda saw that Pantu was not badly hurt, he began to chop up his tree. He found a place where the trunk was smooth and round; he chopped off two sections, each about a foot wide. He smoothed them off and made a hole through the centre. So his wheel was really just a slice across the tree with a hole in the centre for the axle. Oshda spent several days making the wheel, and Pantu went out with him every day.

"There, Pantu, you may roll one of the new wheels home," said Oshda at last.

Oshda lifted the wheel up on its edge, and Pantu began to roll it along down the hills. Soon he grew careless, and the wheel slipped and fell down flat, hitting one of his toes. It was heavy and hurt him.

"Ouch!" said Pantu. Then he stopped short.

"You careless boy," said Oshda. "First you run under a falling tree and almost get killed. Then you let your wheel fall down on your toes. You must be more careful."

"I'll try," said Pantu, hopping about on one foot and holding the hurt one in his hand.

So Oshda tipped the wheel up on its edge again, and this time Pantu was very careful and rolled it safely home without letting it slip.

Their father, Docas, met them as they came home. It was almost supper time, and he had come out to see if they were near. He looked at the bump on Pantu's head, at his skinned knee, and at his bruised toes. He knew that Pantu had not been paying attention to what he was about.

Pantu looked up at his father. Docas looked gravely at him, so Pantu hung his head a little and limped into the house.

Then Docas looked at Oshda and smiled. "He'll learn not to be so careless by the time he gets a few more bumps," said Oshda, smiling.

SHIPPING THE HIDES AND TALLOW.

NEXT morning Oshda put his new wheels on the old cart. He then got two oxen and brought them in front of the cart. He put a strong, heavy piece of wood across just behind the horns of the oxen and fastened it to their horns with rawhide. Then he hitched this wooden yoke to the cart, piled the cart full of skins, and they were ready to go.

Pantu said, " Oh, father, may I go too? I could attend to the soap-suds."

" Yes, you may go," said Docas.

Oshda brought out a pail of very thick soap-suds and set it down in the corner of the cart. He also put in some soap to make more suds when that was gone.

At last they started. Oshda and Docas walked along by the side of the oxen, and poked them with sharp sticks to make them go. Pantu sat up in front of the load of dry hides. As they started out, the cart jolted, the dry hides crackled, and the axle squeaked. It made such a noise that Father Catala, who was in the field half a mile away, heard them coming.

When they came up to him, he said, " You had better put some more soap-suds in the axle holes. I heard the squeaking when you first started out."

So Pantu poured some more soap-suds on the axle.

A number of other carts were going along filled also with hides and with tallow. Docas was in charge of the whole party. They travelled all day and camped at night, and by the evening of the third day they were at Monterey.

They camped just outside of Monterey, and on the next day they went up into the town. They were wandering around, when suddenly they heard the cry of "Sail ho!" In a few seconds every one was calling "Sail ho!" and running down to the beach.

Pantu stood on the beach. It was evening, and the sun was down near the water. After a few moments he saw a little white spot far out on the water. Docas said it was the sails of the ship. There was a blazing path from the sun to the shore, so that Pantu had to shade his eyes, and even then he could not look long at the glowing water. But all of a sudden the sun seemed to sink into the water, and the glow faded.

"Oh, father!" called Pantu to Docas, "the sun has dropped into the ocean and the water has put it out."

"Don't be afraid. It will come up again as bright and hot as ever to-morrow morning," said Docas.

Little by little the ship came nearer. Pantu

stood watching it until it grew so dark that he could no longer see even the white gleam of the sails. Docas and Oshda had been gone a long time. But still he stayed down at the beach, although it was long past supper time.

"Come, Pantu, you must come home," he heard Oshda saying at last.

"But I want to see the big ship come up on the beach," said Pantu.

Oshda laughed. Then he said, "It will not come anywhere near the shore."

Pantu said, "How can we get the heavy hides and tallow into the ship if it stays away off there?"

"It can't come nearer. The water is not deep enough. But they will send some little boats ashore in the morning. We shall load the hides into them, and they will carry them out to the ship," answered Oshda.

In the morning, Pantu was down on the beach very early. Soon he saw a boat leave the ship and come toward the shore. When a big wave came rolling up, the men in the boat rowed very hard. The wave brought them high up on the beach, then, as it began to run back again, the men jumped out into the water, seized the boat, and kept it from being washed back into the bay again. They fastened it so that no wave could wash it away; then they began to load the hides.

Docas and Oshda brought the hides and tallow down to the beach in the ox carts.

•

Docas and Oshda brought the hides and tallow down to the beach in the ox-carts.

All the sailors had on thick woollen caps. Pantu
wondered why they wore that kind of cap, until
he saw how they carried the hides.

A man came up on the dry sand where Docas
and Oshda had piled the hides. He took up a
hide and put it on his head. He waded out
through the water, put the hide into the boat,
and came back for another.

Soon all the men in the boat, except the two
that held it from being tipped over, were running back and forth, carrying hides. The men
had to be very careful not to get the hides wet, for
they would spoil if they became damp. The
sharp stones cut the men's feet, but shoes could
not be worn because the salt water would soon
spoil them.

After the boat was loaded, the man who steered
stood up in the stern. Two of the men got into
the boat and took their oars ready to row. Two
other men stood by the side of the boat to push
it out when the time came. They waited until a
big wave floated the boat; then the man who was
steering said, " Now ! "

The men outside seized hold of the boat, and
ran out with it until the water was above their
waists. Then they tumbled over into the boat
and lay in the bottom, dripping wet.

The men at the oars pulled as hard as they could, but it was of no use. A bigger wave came and swept the boat up high on the beach.

The two men jumped out and turned the boat around so that its end pointed out to sea, and waited to try again. When a large wave came, they again ran out with the boat, and tumbled in after they got to deep water.

But the big waves came so close together that the boat was tossed up and down in the air. Sometimes a big breaker would roll out from under the boat, and let it drop on the water so hard that it seemed as if the bottom would be broken in. Finally, a big curling wave came. The boat was washed around sideways. The swell tipped the boat up, and then partly broke over it.

In a moment more, the boat was upset, and hides, men and oars were mixed up in the foaming water. They were all washed up high on the sand a second time. But now these hides were wet, so they must be stretched out in the sun to dry, and the boat must be loaded with some other hides and tallow.

The third time the men said: "We shall succeed this time. The seventh big wave is the last of the big ones for a while. We will wait for it."

So they waited until six big waves had gone by. When the seventh came, a quick run and a hard

pull carried them beyond the reach of the break·
ers, and they were safe.

"Do they always have such hard times getting
off?" asked Pantu of a white man standing near.

"No," said the man; "the waves are unusually
high to-day."

TRADING ON THE SHIP.

AFTER the hides and tallow had been sent up
to the ship, the captain said that the people
could come aboard and trade.

The Father from the Carmel Mission near
Monterey said he was going to visit the ship.
He took some of his own Mission Indians with
him. Docas, Oshda, and Pantu went along also
to trade for their Mission.

The sailors took them out in one of the boats.
As the Father went on board the ship, the captain gave orders to fire the big guns of the ship
as a salute to him; then the sailors showed the
visitors all over the ship. Pantu was much
interested. He thought, "If only we Indians
could have boats and ships to sail about in instead of just tule-boats!"

At last the captain took them down into the
trading-room. All around it were shelves, on
which the goods were laid out. Father Catala
had told Docas to bring a great many shoes and

As the Father went on board the ship, the captain gave orders to
fire the big guns as a salute to him.

axes for the Mission, so he bought those first. Then the captain said, "You brought so many hides you can still have some more things."

At first, Docas did not know what to take. There were so many new and beautiful things spread out before him. Soon he saw a round, flat, thick thing, about as big as a cake of tallow, with a hole through the middle of it.

"What is it?" he asked.

"It's a grindstone to sharpen your axes with," answered the captain.

He showed Docas how to put a sharp edge on the axe with the grindstone, so Docas said he would take two of them. Docas also got some beads and a toothbrush for Pantu.

After the Father had finished his trading, they all got into the boat again, and the sailors started to row them back to the shore. When they were a little way from the ship, the sailors stopped rowing and rested, while the men on the ship fired a parting salute to the Mission Father.

All this time Pantu had been holding his toothbrush tightly in one hand. He was so happy to think that he was going to brush his teeth just as the little white boys did. As soon as they got to land, he jumped out and ran to the creek. He dipped the brush into the water, and he rubbed and rubbed his teeth with it. He rubbed so hard that the blood came.

" It isn't so much fun as I thought it would be," he said to himself.

On the next day they started for home, and Pantu had many things to tell Colla.

LEAVING THE MISSION.

BUMPTY–BUMP went the ox-cart as it rolled along on the wheels that had not been smoothed off perfectly round.

Creakity-creak went the dry axles, saying as plainly as they could, " We want some more soap-suds. We want some more soap-suds."

Wobblety-jerk went the head of a small Indian girl who sat in the cart on some skin sacks filled with grain. With her were an old man and a boy a little older than herself. Finally her head gave an extra big jerk and hit against one of the posts at the side.

" Just like a girl to fall asleep and then bump her head," said the boy. He straightened him-self up and drew an old woollen cloth around his shoulders in imitation of the cloak worn by a Spanish gentleman who passed them on horse-back just then.

The Spanish gentleman was Don Secundini Robles, who for years had been superintendent of the Santa Clara Mission. The old man in the cart was Docas, and the boy and girl were his grandchildren. Their parents were Oshda and his wife Putsha. The girl's name was Yappa, and the boy's was Shecol. Don Secundini had bought a large ranch about sixteen miles north of the Mission and was going there to live. Docas and his family were going to live with him and be his servants.

"I'm so tired riding in this old ox-cart," said Yappa at last.

"You would be more tired if you had to walk all the way, as I did sixty years ago when we went to the Mission to live," said Docas.

"Why didn't you ride?" asked Yappa.

"We had never seen an ox-cart then," answered Docas.

"Tell us about the time when you were young, grandpa," said Shecol.

So Docas began and told them stories about the life at the old rancheria, and the fight with the Indians from the other rancheria. He told how they were saved by Father Pena from torture and how they went to live at the Mission. Then, he told them about the building of the big church, about the planting of the grainfields and orchards, about the thousands and thousands of cattle and horses that belonged to the Mission, and about the hundreds of Indians who lived under the care of the good Fathers. "Our Mission is not now what it used to be," said Docas, sadly.

With her were an old man and a little boy.

"What happened to the Mission?" Yappa asked.

"The Mexican government took away the lands and then the Indians left. Some have gone back to live at the old rancherias, and some, like ourselves, are going to live with rich Spaniards," answered Docas.

Just then the cart stopped, and they all got out at their new home.

"Aren't you glad the house is not built yet?" Shecol asked Yappa. "We shall have to camp out all the summer and we can play we are wild Indians again."

So the children trapped fish and gathered acorns for bread just as their grandfather told them he used to do. Docas was too old to work much, but their father and older brother, Occano, helped Don Secundini build the big adobe house near which Docas was to spend the rest of his life.

PART III.

WHEN DOCAS LIVED WITH DON SECUNDINI
ROBLES.

PART III.

WHEN DOCAS LIVED WITH DON SECUNDINI ROBLES.

WASH-DAY.

" WE must soap the ox-cart well to-night, Occano," said Oshda to his oldest son.

" What does the Señor Robles want us to do to-morrow ? " asked Occano.

" It is not the Señor that wants us to-morrow. It is the Señora. Now that the sun has come again, we are all going to start for the creek very early in the morning to have a wash-day," said Oshda.

Next morning, before it was daylight, the oxen were yoked to the cart, and lunch was stowed away inside. Then Donna Maria, as they called the Señora Robles, climbed into the cart with her five children. Oshda and Occano walked by the side of the oxen.

There were five horses with soiled clothes piled up high on their backs, led by Pantu and other of the Indian menservants. Putsha, Colla, and other Indian women who were going to wash the clothes walked along by the side of the horses. Shecol and Yappa went too.

Before it was light, as they went slowly along, they heard the howling of the coyotes and other wild animals. The Spanish children crept closer to Donna Maria then, while Shecol and Yappa held on to Putsha's skirts as they walked along.

As it grew light and the animals stopped howling, Donna Maria let the children get down from the cart and run along picking flowers with Shecol and Yappa. Such fun as they had climbing up the hillsides, gathering whole handfuls of the first shooting-stars and buttercups!

Once they all tried to run down a steep hill to see which one would be the first to get to a stray poppy that had blossomed earlier than the others. Shecol was ahead, but just as he reached the poppy, he caught his foot in a gopher hole and fell. The oldest Spanish boy was close behind, and he fell over Shecol. Yappa fell on top of him. The four other children were coming so fast that they could not stop, so they were all piled in a heap.

They got on their feet again as soon as they could, and Yappa said, "Shecol and the poppy must be crushed entirely." But when Shecol could be seen again they found that he was

Colla, Putsha, and the other women put soap on the clothes; then they dipped them into the creek.

laughing, and that he had happened to throw his arm around the poppy, so that it was not hurt.

Just then they heard Donna Maria's voice calling, " Come, children.   You will get left behind," so they started off again on a run to catch up with the cart.   Shecol gave the poppy to Yappa to carry; then he turned somersaults all the way down to the foot of the hill.

When they got to the cart, they filled Donna Maria's lap with flowers.   The smaller children were tired, so they sat in the back of the cart, with their feet hanging over behind.

The children all liked to have the wash-day come, for it was like one big picnic for them.

By and by they came to the creek.   The men took the loads off the horses and unyoked the oxen.   Then they turned them all loose to graze on the wild oats.   The children helped the women carry the baskets of soiled clothes down to the rocks.

Colla, Putsha, and the other women put soap on the clothes.   Then they dipped them into the creek and rubbed them on the rocks in the creek bed.   This made the clothes very white, for the wash-water was always clean and fresh.

By noon the clothes were all washed, and the children had spread them out on the tops of the bushes to dry.   Then came lunch.   " How good everything tastes!" said Yappa. "We are so hungry."

In the afternoon they all rested and played. By evening the clothes were dry, and everything was made ready to start for home again.

The Spanish children were all tired, so they crowded down near their mother in the cart. There was a little room left in the cart, and they begged that Shecol and Yappa might come in with them instead of walking all the way home. Donna Maria said "Yes," so Shecol and Yappa nestled down in a corner of the cart.

Yappa was sleepy, and she leaned her head against Shecol's shoulder. As the sun went down, the Indians began to sing "Kyrie Eleison." She whispered to Shecol, "That's the song grandpa sang when he was a little boy, and Father Serra visited the Mission."

"Yes," said Shecol.

The cart jolted along. The Indians kept on singing. A red moon came up over the mountains. A flock of wild ducks whizzed by just over their heads. The frogs began to croak in the little ponds near the road, and the crickets began to sing in the long grass.

Yappa fell asleep and dreamed that she was a little cricket and that she was trying to learn to sing "Kyrie Eleison," but that it was such hard work, because, every time she tried to sing, all

she could say was " Katy Do." She felt very
badly, for she dreamed that Father Serra was
coming toward her and that he wanted to hear
her sing.

Soon she thought that Father Serra stood before her, and said, " I am Father Serra. Will you
sing for me ? "

She answered, " I will try, Father," and began.
But all she could say was " Katy Do," so she
stopped.

" I am so sorry, Father, I tried to sing ' Kyrie
Eleison,' " she said.

" You have done well, dear girl," said the Father.
" You sang your own song the best you could."
Then he smiled at her and put his arm round her.

She woke up just then and found that they were
at home, and that her father Oshda had her in his
arms and was smiling down at her as he carried
her into the house.

THE CASCARONE BALL.

" THE old white hen has stolen her nest, and
Donna Maria says we must go and hunt for
the eggs this morning," said Shecol to Yappa one
day.

" All right," said Yappa. " But why doesn't
Donna Maria let that hen have some little

chickens? We have brought her so many eggs lately."

" Don't you know why Donna Maria wants so many eggs these days?" asked Shecol.

" No," said Yappa.

" Why, we are going to have a cascarone ball here next week," said Shecol.

" Oh, goody!" said Yappa, clapping her hands.

They started off on a run and hunted every-where· for the nests, — down under the bushes, around the sheds, and out in the garden. At last, when they had given up in despair and were running home through the orchard, the old white hen jumped up with a startled cackle. She was almost under their feet.

" Be careful, Yappa. You will step on the nest," said Shecol.

The children stopped short and began to peep about in the long grass. Soon they saw a little hollow with eleven eggs in it. Shecol had brought a basket with him, and they put the eggs into that and then carried them back carefully to the house.

That evening the Indians all gathered at Oshda's house. Putsha brought out a basket filled with eggs. Putsha took one and said, "Watch me, Shecol and Yappa, so that you can do it, too."

She made a hole in each end of the egg; then she put her mouth to one hole and blew all the inside part of the egg out into a dish.

While Putsha was blowing the egg, Colla ran up to the Robles' house. Soon she came back carrying a large bowl of perfumed water in her hands. Putsha put the eggshell into the bowl, and the perfumed water ran into the shell through the holes in the ends. When it was partly full, Putsha lifted the egg out and dropped some melted wax on each of the holes in the ends. In a few minutes the wax hardened, and Yappa held in her hand what seemed to be an egg. But it was really an eggshell half filled with perfumed water.

"Won't the people smell sweet when they get these eggs broken on their heads!" said Yappa.

Putsha, Colla, and the children worked hard that evening before they had all the eggs blown and filled.

The next night Putsha brought out another basket of eggs, but instead of perfumed water to fill them with, Donna Maria sent a basket of gold and silver paper, cut into tiny bits. The paper was a brittle, crackly kind that glistened in the light. Some of these eggs they colored red, some blue, some red and yellow, and some were spotted.

After the eggs were ready, the cooking began, and for two or three days the Indian women were busy at that. The Robles had invited all their friends from San José, and from all the country around. They knew that their guests would be very hungry after riding so far.

"Let's go to meet them."

The ball was to be on Wednesday evening. Wednesday morning Shecol heard a great noise of shouting and laughing toward the south.

"They're coming, Yappa. Let's go to meet them," he called.

When the children had run out a little way, they could see some people coming—about twenty-five in the party. These were the Spanish guests and their Indian servants. They were having great fun, for the men were fine riders. They could bend down from their saddles and pick flowers from the ground as they galloped past.

"I wonder what they are doing when they ride up against each other," said Yappa. As they came nearer she saw that they were smearing each other's faces with bright colors. Such looking people as they were! But as that was all part of the fun, no one cared.

The Robles family took their friends inside the house to wash their faces, while some of the Indian servants came to where Oshda lived.

"Oh, grandpa, here's Yisoo's son," called Yappa to Docas as one of the Indians stopped at their door.

Yappa could not stay to listen to what they said, for she had to hurry and help her mother with supper. The long tables were set out in an arbor near the house.

In the evening came the ball, for which the

largest room in the house had been cleared. Yappa and Shecol climbed up outside one of the windows where they could see everything that went on.

As soon as the people began to gather, came the fun of smashing the eggs on each other's heads. Don Secundini Robles was standing in the crowd talking to one of his friends from San José, when Donna Maria came up behind him and smashed an eggshell filled with perfumed water on his head. Then she jumped back among the crowd before he could turn round to see who did it.

Every one laughed, for the scented water was running down all over his face and dripping off the end of his nose. Soon the guests looked as if they had silver and gold hair, so many of the paper cascarones had been broken on their heads.

By and by all the eggs were gone. Donna Maria saw Shecol sitting in the window.

" Run and get some napkins and some water," she called to him.

" Come, Yappa," he said, jumping down from the window and holding up his arms to help his sister. They ran to the kitchen and came back loaded. Putsha helped them carry in the pails of water.

As soon as the guests inside saw the water, they gave a shout. They dipped the napkins in the water and began to slap each other with the wet napkins.

Antonio, one of the men, slipped out and came back with a glass tumbler, and after that when any one slapped him with a napkin he threw a tumbler of water at him. By and by he threw a tumbler of water squarely in the face of Pedro. Pedro seized the bucket of water and threw the whole of it over Antonio. Everybody in the room laughed at Pedro and Antonio, and the water-throwing stopped.

By this time every one was tired, so they rested a little. Then the musicians started to play, and the real dance began.

Putsha and Shecol and Yappa went to bed soon after the dancing began, but the Spaniards danced until morning.

.

THE SHEEP-SHEARING.

" HOW hot I am!" said Shecol to Yappa, taking off his big hat and fanning himself with it.

" What have you been doing?" asked Yappa.

" Driving the sheep into the pens," said Shecol. " The shearing begins to-morrow."

" I should think the sheep would be glad to get rid of their wool these warm days," said Yappa, who was grinding corn.

" You had better hurry up with your tortillas.

The shearers will be here in a little while. They have just finished shearing the sheep at the San Francisquito ranch," said Shecol.

Soon the band of shearers came, and shortly after they arrived, supper was served to them under the spreading grape vines a little way from the house.

Yisoo's son, Kole, was captain of the band of twenty shearers. It was made up of Indians from the old Santa Clara Mission.

As soon as supper was over, the shearers went down to the creek and came back with their arms filled with willow boughs, which Kole had them make into a number of brush huts. They slept in these while they were at the Robles ranch.

Oshda, Occano, and Pantu had been out for two days gathering together the sheep belonging to the Robles, and now there were five thousand sheep waiting in the pens, wondering what was going to happen to them.

A big shed had been built for the shearers to stand under while they worked.

Long before the shearers were up, Shecol was sitting on the fence and looking at the sheep.

"Where are you going to put the wool when it is cut off the sheep?" he asked his father, as Oshda came toward the pens.

"The men will toss the fleeces up to me, and I shall throw them down into this big bag. When

the bag gets pretty well filled, I shall have to jump
up and down on the fleeces so that we can get as
many into the bag as possible," answered Oshda.
He climbed up one of the posts of the shed and
stood ready for work by a large bag that was
hanging in a frame at the edge of the roof.

In a few minutes more the shearers came and
the work began. Pantu stood by a table, and
every time a shearer brought a fleece to the table,
Pantu gave him a five-cent piece.

Soon Yappa came out also to watch the shearing, but as hour after hour went by, the sun rose
higher and higher, and the air grew hot and was
filled with dust. By and by Yappa said, " I'm
tired of watching them, Shecol. Let's go and
build a brush hut for ourselves with some of the
willow branches that were left over from the
shearers' huts."

" All right," said Shecol. " We'll play that we
are wild Indians living out on a rancheria as
grandpa used to do."

In a little while the hut was built.

" Now I'm going to make a mat out of some of
those tules you brought from the bay yesterday,"
said Yappa.

" I'll go out hunting, while you make the mats,"
said Shecol, tying some string to a willow stick
to make a bow to play with.

But just then Putsha called, " Come, Yappa,

Shecol lifted the lamb carefully in his arms and carried it toward the hut.

you must help me with the tortillas," and their play was broken up.

After dinner, Shecol and Yappa went down to the shearing place again to see what was going on. As they came near, Oshda said, " Do you want a lamb ? "

" Yes," shouted Shecol and Yappa in the same breath. " Where is it ? "

" Out at the end of the shed. Its leg is broken, and you may have it if you will take care of it."

But they scarcely heard the last words he said, they were running so fast for the lamb.

" Poor little lamb ! " said Yappa, as they bent over it.

" We'll bind up its leg first," said Shecol, getting some sticks for splints. He pulled some string out of his pocket and bound the splints on as well as he could.

" Now we'll put it into the hut we made," said Yappa.

Shecol lifted the lamb carefully in his arms and carried it toward the hut.

" Be careful. You are hurting it," said Yappa. She placed her hand under the lamb, and put the wounded leg, which was hanging down, up in its proper place.

" I'll run ahead," said Yappa, " and get a pile of soft tule rushes ready for you to put it down on."

In a few minutes more the lamb was lying

on the rushes in the cool shade of the willow boughs.

" We must bring it some water," said Shecol.

" Yes, and let's name it Yisoo, after grandpa's friend," said Yappa.

The shearers stayed several days longer, but the children did not watch them any more, for they were taking care of their pet lamb.

THE BARBECUE.

" WHERE'S father?" asked Yappa of her mother one afternoon.

" Gone off with Don Secundini to dig the pits for the barbecue," answered Putsha.

" And where's Shecol?"

" He has gone with them," said Putsha. " But we must go to work, for we have bread to make and corn to get ready for tortillas to-day. The corn is all ready for you to grind. It has been soaked in the limewater. Begin to grind it while I build a fire in the oven."

Yappa went over to what the Mexicans called a metate, and sitting down on the ground began to grind the corn. The metate was a big, smooth stone with two legs on one end of it. The legs made it stand up slanting. Yappa put some corn on the metate and ground it with another smooth stone.

Putsha built a fire in the big brick oven at the back of the house. She then came near where Yappa was at work, and began to make the bread. When the fire had made the oven very hot, she went to it, scraped the fire all out, and pushed the bread in on the hot bricks. Then she closed the oven door and left the bread until it was baked.

When the bread was in the oven, she said to Yappa, "Hurry, Yappa, and build a fire. Shecol will be back soon and he will be hungry. We must have some tortillas ready for him."

"Isn't father coming too?" asked Yappa.

"No; he will have to stay all night to turn the meat so that it does not burn," answered Putsha.

Putsha put some big, smooth stones into the fire she had built outside on the ground. Then she brought some grease and rubbed it well into the cornmeal, so that the little grains of cornmeal all stuck together and made a paste.

By this time, the stone Putsha had put into the fire was very hot, so she pulled it out a little to one side and spread some of the batter over it. In a little while one side of the tortilla was brown, so Putsha turned it over to cook on the other side. Just as it was cooked Shecol came hurrying up.

"Anything to eat?" he asked.

The tortilla was just done, so Yappa gave it to

Yappa grinding corn

him.   He rolled it up like a jelly roll and began eating it.

"It's good.   Any more?" he asked between bites.

"In a few minutes," answered Putsha.   She had pulled out some more stones and was cooking more tortillas.

"What have you been doing, Shecol?" asked Yappa, as they waited for the other tortillas to cook.

"Digging a pit to cook the meat," answered Shecol.

Next morning Donna Maria and three other women who were visiting her, got into one of the ox-carts, which was decorated with boughs and flowers.   A second cart was standing near, and all Donna Maria's children climbed into it.

This cart was lined with hides so that it was not only comfortable, but safe, for the hides kept the children from falling out.   Putsha and Colla rode in this cart also, in order to take care of the children.   A third cart was loaded so heavily with roast turkeys, chickens, corn-tamales, bread, and other things to eat, that it went "squeakity-squeak," as it rolled along.

When everything was ready, Occano and some of the other drivers pushed the oxen with the ends of their long poles, and they began to move slowly away.   The Indians walked along by the sides of the carts just as they did on wash-day, but this time all the men went as well as the women. Most of the men rode on horseback. One man played a violin, while another man rode behind him to guide the horse.

When they came to the place where the barbecue was to be held, Shecol took Yappa all round and showed her the meat cooking. As they walked along they saw Oshda.

" There's father!" cried Yappa.

" Yes," said Shecol, " he has been up here all night, turning the meat over to keep it from burning."

As they came nearer Yappa saw a big pit in the ground about ten feet long. This was lined with stones. An ox had been cut in half and some long iron skewers stuck through the halves; then the oxen were hung across the top of the pit. Yappa gave a sniff.

" It smells good," she said. " It's getting brown too," and she peered down into the pit at the glowing coals below.

They passed a place where some men had begun to dig in the ground.

" That's where the head is cooking," said Shecol.

" Down there in the ground?" exclaimed Yappa.

" Yes, we dug a little hole, lined it with stones, and built a fire. After the stones were very hot, we raked the fire out, scattered some dirt over the stones so that they should not burn the meat, and set the head right down in it; then we filled the hole with dirt."

Don Secundini came up just as the men finished taking the head out of the hole. He brushed off the dirt and said, "This is the best of all the meat." He took it over where Donna Maria was sitting and said to her, "You shall have the tongue."

"Thank you," said Donna Maria.

"I don't think I ever tasted such good meat before," said Yappa.

"It is so juicy and tender," said Shecol.

Yappa looked around at the long tables. Then she said, "What a crowd there is!"

"No wonder," answered Shecol. "The Robles have invited everybody from San José to San Francisco. See! There are Señor Soto and Señor Sanchez and Señor Martinez!"

After the people had finished eating, Yappa said, "Now what shall we do?"

"The men are going to ride on their horses and play games," answered Shecol.

HORSEBACK-RIDING.

AFTER the people had finished eating, Don Secundini rode out in front of them. He leaned over from the saddle and picked up a leaf from the ground as he galloped along.

"Well done, Don Secundini!" said Don Francisco. "Here is a rooster for us to practise on to-day."

As they came closer, Shecol saw the head of a live rooster sticking out of the ground. Just then he heard a shout and saw the oldest son of Señor Soto come on a gallop toward the rooster. As he passed the rooster, he leaned down and tried to seize it by the head, but he missed it. All the people laughed, and young Soto laughed too, as he turned his horse around and came back where they were.

"Better luck next time," he said.

Pedro then tried to seize the head, but he, too, missed.

"You boys cannot ride so well as your fathers yet," said Señor Sanchez. "Many a time have I seen Don Secundini ride for the rooster, and never yet have I seen him fail." At this he seized Pedro playfully by the leg and pulled him down out of the saddle. Then he added, "Show the boys how it should be done, Señor Robles."

So Don Secundini rode away a little distance, and then came galloping back. Suddenly he bent down, and in a moment more was holding the kicking, flopping rooster up in the air.

"Bueno, bueno!" they all cried.

"Let's have the game of rods," said the Señor Martinez. All the men and boys were on horseback, so they made a ring with the horses facing inward. Señor Soto rode around the outside of the ring with a thick stick in his hand. Soon he passed the stick to Pedro and then rode quickly away. Pedro chased him as fast as his horse could go, for if he caught up it was fair for him to whip the Señor Soto over the back with the stick.

Several times Pedro came very close to Señor Soto, but the Señor would give his horse a sudden pull and turn quickly to one side, so that Pedro could not hit him. Once, however, the Señor, instead of dodging, turned around to see how far away Pedro was. In a moment more Pedro was close beside him whipping him as fast as he could.

One of the blows happened to hit the Señor's horse by mistake, and the horse gave such a jump that Señor Soto was able to get in Pedro's old place in the ring before he could catch up again. Then the Señor was safe, and Pedro had to give the stick to some one else and be chased in turn.

By and by it was home time. Shecol was playing near and Pedro noticed him look wistfully at them as they turned to ride away.

" Would you like to go with us ? " Pedro asked.

" Yes, I would," was Shecol's answer.

" But how could you take him? He can't ride yet," said Don Secundini.

Don Secundini.

"I could put him on a blanket on the ground and tie the blanket to my saddle with a lasso, the way Antonio does with his little brother," said Pedro. "Run off and tell your mother while I get the blanket," continued Pedro.

In a few minutes they had started. At first Pedro went very slowly and carefully, for fear Shecol would tumble off, but after a little, Shecol said, "You may go faster if you like. I can stick on all right." So Pedro let his horse begin to gallop.

Suddenly he heard a shout. He looked around and saw Shecol sitting on the ground quite a distance behind. The blanket was bumping over the ground at his horse's heels. He stopped his horse and waited until Shecol caught up with him, and after that he went more slowly, for he did not want to lose Shecol again.

THE RODEO.

"IS it going to rain? Look at that big cloud," said Yappa to Shecol one afternoon in June.

"I hope it will not rain to-day," said Shecol, "for you know we are going to have a round-up of the cattle and then a barbecue afterward." In a moment more he added, "I know; it's a dust cloud that the cattle are making as the men drive them along."

"Come on, then; we shall just have time to climb the tree by the corral," said Yappa, starting off to run.

Shecol followed after, and in a few minutes they were both safely seated on the branch of a large live-oak tree near the corral.

"I do hope we can find our calf again," said Yappa. "You know Don Secundini said when he gave it to us last year that we could not keep it unless we could tell it when we saw it this year."

"Oh, I think we shall know it," answered Shecol. "Remember the white spots on its forehead and on its left hip."

Soon a number of men came riding out toward the corrals. The servants rode off to help drive the cattle, while Don Secundini, Don Francisco, Señor Soto, Señor Sanchez, and Señor Martinez halted their horses just under the tree where Shecol and Yappa were sitting.

"We shall have a fine place to see from," said Shecol.

The men below them looked up when they heard a voice above. Don Secundini laughed. Then he said, "Don't fall down, little ones. These cattle aren't used to children, and they might hurt you."

"We're going to look for our calf," said Shecol.

In a few minutes Yappa said, "There they come!"

Shecol peeped out from among the leaves and saw Oshda and Pantu driving a little bunch of cattle toward them.

As the bunch came nearer, Don Francisco said, "There are two of my cattle. I see my brand on the hip."

One of Don Francisco's men rode up, separated his two cattle from the others and drove them to one side. The rest of that bunch belonged to Don Secundini, so they drove the calves into a corral where they could be branded. The old ones they drove off in another direction.

As the second bunch came near them, Yappa saw a little calf running along with one of Don Secundini's cows. The calf had a white spot on its forehead and one on its left hip. Yappa gave Shecol a pull and said, "There it is."

"Where?" asked Shecol.

Yappa pointed it out, but Shecol said, "That can't be our calf. That's the way our calf looked last year. It will have grown to be very large by this time, and besides, father branded it with Don Secundini's brand. This calf has no brand yet."

They looked over every bunch that came by, hoping to find their calf. At last, as their eyes were beginning to get tired, Shecol said, "Don Secundini, look at that calf at the head of the bunch that is coming. That's ours."

Don Secundini looked at the calf, then he said, " Yes, Shecol, it is yours. You have won the calf."

The herders kept on bringing up bunch after bunch of cattle and letting each owner pick out those that belonged to him. The cattle had been running wild for so many months that those from the different ranches were all mixed.

There were so many to look over that their herds were not nearly sorted out by evening, so, while some of the men drove home the neighbors' cattle, others prepared to keep the main herd together all night.

" And now how are you youngsters going to get home?" asked Don Secundini, as he gathered up his bridle-reins ready to ride back to the house.

" Aren't they going to drive the cattle away from here?" asked Shecol.

" Not until to-morrow evening. I'll speak to your father about you," said Don Secundini.

When Oshda saw where they were, he rode up to the tree. He said, " You cannot walk home through these cattle. Drop down behind me on my horse."

First Yappa, then Shecol, dropped down on the horse. Yappa put her arms around Oshda, and Shecol put his arms around Yappa. In this way they did not fall off as they rode home.

After supper Oshda said, " Good-by. I have to watch with the cattle until midnight."

The cattle were restive, for they were in a strange place. All of a sudden an owl gave a screech from a tree in the midst of the herd. The cattle became frightened and began to run toward Oshda. There were so many of them and they were coming so fast that Oshda knew he would be run over if he rode toward them, so he turned his horse and rode as fast as he could ahead of them.

When he got a little ahead, he began to turn the herd toward the left. He did not try to turn the whole big herd at once, but only to make the front ones run crosswise. The other herders helped him, and soon more of the cattle began to run toward the left.

After a little the whole herd were running round in a circle. The herders let the cattle run round and round as long as they liked, but by and by the cattle got so dusty and tired and dizzy that they stopped running of their own accord. The herders then drove them back again, for they were no longer afraid.

When the cattle were safely back, Oshda said, "We must keep singing or whistling all night. That will let the cattle know that some one is near them, and they will not be so easily frightened."

So all the rest of the night the darkness was filled with the sound of singing, and the cattle were quiet. Oshda and the herders with him watched until midnight; then others came out to relieve them.

Meanwhile, the people at the Robles' adobe had been having a gay time, for they had a barbecue under the spreading grape vines when they first went to the house, and in the evening they had a dance.

Next morning the work with the cattle began again, and all day every one was busy. At the end of that time, the cattle belonging to the different ranches were separated, the calves were branded with the special mark of the owners, and the cattle were all turned out to roam again.

FOR A CONCLUSION.

AND so Docas lived his life, — as a small boy at the Indian rancheria, as a larger boy and man at the Mission, and as an old man with his children and grandchildren about him at the home of Don Secundini. He was a very old man when he went to the Robles' home, for it was in 1769 that the first white man came to the rancheria, and it was 1849 before Don Secundini built the big adobe ranch house. His life of mingled play and work is ended, and therefore ended also is the story of Docas, the Indian boy of Santa Clara.

BIBLIOGRAPHY.

BALLARD, ROY. Don Secundini Robles. In *Sequoia*, Stanford University. Sept. 13, 1894. p. 16.

BANCROFT, H. H. The Native Races. Vol. IV., Antiquities. San Francisco: The History Co. 1886. pp. x + 807.

—— The Works of. Vol. XXXIV., California Pastoral. San Francisco: The History Co. 1888. pp. vi + 808.

BARNES, M. S. The Robles Rancheria. In *Sequoia*, Stanford University. Sept. 13, 1894. pp. 15–16.

BEECHEY, CAPT. F. W. Narrative of a Voyage to the Pacific and Bering's Strait. London: Henry Colburn and Richard Bentley. 1831. Vol. II. pp. iv + 451.

BENNETT, JOHN E. Should the California Missions be Preserved? In *Overland Monthly*. San Francisco. Feb. 1897. pp. 150–161.

BERNAL, IGNACIO. Memories of the Santa Clara Valley. In *Sequoia*, Stanford University. Feb. 21, 1896. pp. 292–294.

BIDWELL, JOHN. Life in California before the Gold Discovery. In *Century*, Vol. XLI. pp. 163–183.

BLACKMAR, FRANK W. Spanish Institutions of the Southwest. Baltimore: The Johns Hopkins Press. 1891. pp. xxv + 353.

BRIONES, BRIGIDA. A Carnival Ball at Monterey in 1829. In *Century*, Vol. XLI. p. 468.

—— A Glimpse of Domestic Life in 1827. In *Century*, Vol. XLI. p. 470.

BRYANT, EDWIN. What I saw in California. New York: D. Appleton and Co. 1849. pp. 480.

CARPENTER, HELEN. Among the Diggers of Thirty Years Ago. In *Overland Monthly*, Feb. 1894. pp. 146.

DANA, RICHARD HENRY. Two Years before the Mast. Boston: James Osgood and Co. 1873. pp. vii + 470.

DE CAMPO, INEZ. El Carpintero. In *Overland Monthly*, Aug. 1895. pp. 211–213.

DOYLE, JOHN T.   The Missions of Alta California.   In *Century*, Vol. XLI.   pp. 389–402.

FASSIN, A. G.   Yuka Legends.   In *Overland Monthly*, June, 1884.   pp. 651–659.

FOOTE, MARY HALLOCK.   The Cascarone Ball.   In *Scribner's*, Aug. 1879.   pp. 615–617.

FORBES, ALEXANDER.   California: A History of Upper and Lower California.   London: Smith, Elder, and Co , Cornhill.   1839.   pp. xvi + 352.

GATES, MARY J.   Contributions to Local History.   San José: Cottle and Murgotten, printers.   1895.   pp. 27.

GREEN, W. S.   The Digger Indian.   In *Overland Monthly*, March, 1895.   pp. 282–284.

HAKLUYT, RICHARD.   The Voyages of the English Nation to America.   Collected by Hakluyt.   Vol. IV.

' HALL, FREDERIC.   History of San José.   San Francisco: A. L. Bancroft and Co.   1871.   pp. xv + 537.

HELPER, HINTON R.   The Land of Gold.   Baltimore: Henry Taylor.   1855.   pp. xii + 200.

HIGUERA, PRUDENCIA.   Trading with the Americans.   In *Century*, Vol. XLI.   pp. 192–193.

HITTELL, JOHN S.   History of the City of San Francisco.   San Francisco: A. L. Bancroft and Co.   1878.   pp. 498.

HITTELL, THEODORE.   History of California.   San Francisco: Pacific Press Pub. House.   1885.   Vol. I.   pp. xxxvi + 799.   Vol. II.   pp. xli + 833.

HUDSON, J. W. · Pomo Basket Makers.   In *Overland Monthly*, June, 1883.

JACKSON, HELEN HUNT.   Father Junipero and his Work.   In *Century*, 1883, May, pp. 3–18 ; June, pp. 199–215.

—— Ramona.   Boston: Roberts Bros.   1886.   pp. 490.

LANGSDORFF, G. H. von.   Voyages and Travels in Various Parts of the World.   London: Henry Colburn.   1814.   Vol. II.

LA PEROUSE, J. T. G.   A Voyage Round the World.   Trans.   London: J. Johnson.   1768.   Vol. II.   pp. x + 498.

L. M.   The Indians of Nevada County.   In *Overland Monthly*, March, 1884.   pp. 275–278.

MILLER, MABEL L.   The So-called California "Diggers."   In *Popular Science Monthly*, Dec. 1896.   pp. 201–214.

PALOU, REV. FRANCIS.   Life of Ven. Padre Junipero Serra.   Trans. by Rev. J. Adam.   San Francisco: P. E. Dougherty.   1884.

POWERS, STEPHEN. Tribes of California. United States Geographical and Geological Survey of the Rocky Mountain Region. Washington. 1877. pp. 635. Also in *Overland Monthly* during the years 1872, 1873, and 1874.

REDDING, B. B. California Indians and their Food. In *Californian*, Nov. 1881. pp. 442–445.

ROBINSON, ALFRED. Life in California. San Francisco: William Doxey. 1891. pp. 284.

ROCQUEFEUILD, CAMILLE DE. Account of California in 1817. In *California Farmer*, Oct. 24, 1862.

SARGENT, LUCY. Indian Dances in Northern California. In *Californian*, May, 1880. pp. 464–469.

SCHOOLCRAFT, H. R. Historical and Statistical Information respecting the Historical Condition and Prospects of the Indian Tribes of the United States. (The title-pages of Vols. IV. and VI. read "Archives of Aboriginal Knowledge.) 6 vols. Philadelphia. 1851–1860.

SHINN, C. H. Pioneer Spanish Families in California. In *Century*. Vol. XLI. pp. 377–389.

SMITHSONIAN REPORT FOR 1886. I. Washington: Government Printing Office. 1889. pp. xiii + 877.

SNEDDEN, DAVID. A Stampede. In *Sequoia*, Stanford University. Oct. 25, 1895.

TAYLOR, ALEX. T. The Indianology of California. In *California Farmer*. Series running through 1861 and 1862.

UNITED STATES. Eleventh Census. Vol. on Indians. Washington: Government Printing Office. 1894. pp. vi + 683.

VALLEJO, GUADALUPE. Ranch and Mission Days in Alta California. In *Century*, Vol. XLI. pp. 183–192.

VANCOUVER, GEORGE. A Voyage of Discovery. London: J. Edwards. *Pall Mall*, 1798. Vol. II. pp. 504.

VASQUEZ, DON PABLO. Don Pablo's Story. In *Sequoia*, Stanford University. May 25, 1892. pp. 331-334.

In addition to the above bibliography much of the material used has been obtained either from personal interviews or from unprinted manuscripts. Especial help was received from Don Pablo Vasquez, the late Mary Sheldon Barnes, Frank Polley, Mrs. J. A. Salaceti, Dane Coolidge, and Antoniette Knowles.

PRONUNCIATION OF NAMES

INDIAN NAMES.

Alachu	.	.	.	.	. Ä lä'chū
Ama .	.	.	.	.	. Ä'mä
Apa .	.	.	.	.	. Ä'pä
Colla .	.	.	.	.	. Kō'lä
Docas .	.	.	.	.	. Dō'käs
Heema	.	.	.	.	. Hē'mä
Keoka .	.	.	.	.	. Kē ō'kä
Kole .	.	.	.	.	. Kō'lā
Massea	.	.	.	.	. Mäs sā'ä
Occano	.	.	.	.	. Ō kä'nō
Oshda .	.	.	.	.	. Ōsh'dä
Pantu .	.	.	.	.	. Pän'tū
Putsha .	.	.	.	.	. Pū'chä
Shecol .	.	.	.	.	. Shē'cōl
Unwa .	.	.	.	.	. Ūm'wä
Yappa .	.	.	.	.	. Yä'pä
Yeeta .	.	.	.	.	. Yē'tä
Yisoo .	.	.	.	.	. Yē'sū

SPANISH WORDS.

Almaden	.	.	.	.	. Äl mä dän'
Antonio	.	.	.	.	. Än tō'nyō
bueno .	.	.	.	.	. bwā'nō
Carmel	.	.	.	.	. Cär mäl'
cascarone	.	.	.	.	. cäs cä rō'nä

Catala	Cā tä'lä
Diego	Dyä'gō
Dolores	Dō lōr'äs
Donna Maria . . .	Dō'na Mä rē'ä
Don Secundini Robles . .	Dōn Sä kŭn dè'nē Rō'bläs
Guadalupe	Gwä dä lū'pä
Junipero Serra . . .	Hūn e pä'rō Sär'rä
metate	mä tä'tä
Monterey	Mōn tä rä'
Pena	Pä'nä
Portola	Pōr tô lä'
rancheria	rän chä rē'ä
rodeo	rō dä'ō
San Francisco . . .	Sän Frän thēs'cō
San Francisquito . . .	San Frän thēs kē'tō
San Jose	Sän Hō sä'
Santa Clara	Sän'tä Clä'ɹä
Señora	Sän nyō'rä
Senor Martinez . . .	Sän'nyōr Mär tē'näz
Senor Sanchez . . .	Sän'nyōr Sän'chäz
Senor Soto	Sän'nyōr Sō'tō
tortillas	tōr tēl'lyas
Tulare	Tū lä'rä
tule	tū'lä